the baby-sitters club®

Kristy's Great Idea

7-4-02

Dearest ███████,
   Have a wonderful
birthday, and enjoy
this wonderful book!
Olove, The ██████████████
                    X
                    O
God bless you now + always!

**Other books by
Ann M. Martin**

Rachel Parker, Kindergarten Show-off
Eleven Kids, One Summer
Ma and Pa Dracula
Yours Turly, Shirley
Ten Kids, No Pets
Slam Book
Just a Summer Romance
Missing Since Monday
With You and Without You
Me and Katie (the Pest)
Stage Fright
Inside Out
Bummer Summer

BABY-SITTERS LITTLE SISTER series
THE BABY-SITTERS CLUB mysteries
THE BABY-SITTERS CLUB series

the babysitters club®

Kristy's Great Idea

ANN M. MARTIN

AN
APPLE
PAPERBACK

SCHOLASTIC INC.
New York Toronto London Auckland Sydney
Mexico City New Delhi Hong Kong Buenos Aires

ISBN 0-439-28424-4

12 11 10 9 8 7 6 5 4 3 2 1   1 2 3 4 5 6/0

Printed in the U.S.A.   40

First Scholastic printing of this revised edition, September 2001

This book is for
Beth McKeever Perkins,
my old baby-sitting buddy.
With love
(and years of memories).

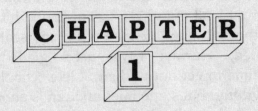

CHAPTER 1

The Baby-sitters Club. I'm proud to say it was totally my idea, even though the four of us worked it out together. "Us" is Mary Anne Spier, Claudia Kishi, Stacey McGill, and me — Kristy Thomas.

I got the idea on the first Tuesday afternoon of seventh grade. It was a very hot day. It was so hot that in my unair-conditioned school, Stoneybrook Middle School, the teachers had opened every single window and door and turned off all the lights. My hair stuck damply to the back of my neck, and I wished I had a rubber band so I could pull it into a long ponytail. Bees flew into the classroom and droned around our heads, and Mr. Redmont, our teacher, let us stop working to make fans out of construction paper. The fans didn't do much except keep the bees away, but it was nice to take up ten minutes of social studies making them.

Anyway, that stifling afternoon dragged on forever, and when the hands of the clock on the front wall of our classroom finally hit 2:42 and the bell rang, I leaped out of my seat and shouted, "Hurray!" I was just so glad that it was time to get out of there. I like school and everything, but sometimes enough is enough.

Mr. Redmont looked shocked. He was probably thinking he'd been so nice letting us make fans and there I was, not appreciating it at all, just glad the day was over.

I felt bad, but I couldn't help what I'd done. I'm like that. I think of something to say, and I say it. I think of something to do, and I do it. Mom calls it impulsive. Sometimes she calls it trouble. But she doesn't just mean trouble. She means *trouble*.

And I was in trouble then. I could sense it. I've been in enough trouble to know when it's coming.

Mr. Redmont cleared his throat. He was trying to think of a way to punish me without humiliating me in front of the other kids. Things like that are important to him.

"Kristy," Mr. Redmont began, and then he changed his mind and started over. "Class," he said, "you have your homework assignments. You may go. Kristy, I'd like to see you for a minute."

While the rest of the kids gathered up their books and papers and left the room, talking and giggling, I made my way up to Mr. Redmont's desk. Before he could say a word, I began apologizing to him. Sometimes that helps.

"Mr. Redmont," I said, "I'm really sorry. I didn't mean anything. I mean, I didn't mean I was glad school was over. I meant I was glad I could go home. Because my house is air-conditioned. . . ."

Mr. Redmont nodded. "But do you think, Kristy, that it would be possible, in the future, for you to conduct yourself with a bit more decorum?"

I wasn't sure of the exact meaning of *decorum*, but I had a pretty good idea it meant not spoiling Mr. Redmont's day by jumping up and shouting hurray when the bell rang.

"Yes, sir," I said. Sometimes being polite also helps.

"Good," said Mr. Redmont. "But I want you to remember this incident, and the best way for us to remember things is to write them down. So tonight, I would like you to write a one-hundred-word essay on the importance of decorum in the classroom."

Darn. I'd have to find out what *decorum* meant after all.

"Yes, sir," I said again.

I went back to my desk, gathered up my books very slowly, and then walked very slowly out of the classroom. I hoped Mr. Redmont was noticing the slowness because I was betting it was an important part of decorum.

I found Mary Anne Spier waiting for me outside the door to my classroom. She was leaning against the wall, biting her nails.

Mary Anne is my best friend. We live next door to each other. We even look a little alike. We're both small for our age and we both have brown hair that falls past our shoulders. But that's where the similarity ends, because I can't keep my mouth shut, and Mary Anne is very quiet and very shy. Luckily, that's only on the outside. The people who know her well, like Claudia and Stacey and me, get to see the inside of her, and the Mary Anne who's hiding in there is a lot of fun.

"Hey," I greeted her. I pulled her hand out of her mouth and looked at her nails. "Mary Anne! How do you ever expect to be able to wear nail polish if you keep doing that?"

"Oh, come on," she said with a sigh. "Nail

polish. I'll be seventy-five before my father lets me wear it."

Mary Anne's father is the only family she's got. Her mother is dead, and she has no brothers or sisters. Unfortunately, her father is pretty strict. My mother says it's just because Mr. Spier is nervous since Mary Anne is all he's got. You'd think, though, that he could let her wear her hair down instead of always in braids, or give her permission to ride her bike to the mall with Claudia and me once in a while. But, no. At Mr. Spier's house it's rules, rules, rules. It's a miracle that Mary Anne was even allowed to become a member of the Baby-sitters Club.

We walked out of school, and suddenly I began running. I forgot all about decorum, because I'd just remembered something else. "Oh, my gosh!" I cried.

Mary Anne raced after me. "What is it?" she panted.

"It's Tuesday," I called over my shoulder.

"So? Slow down, Kristy. It's too hot to run."

"I can't slow down. Tuesday is my afternoon to watch David Michael. I'm supposed to beat him home. Otherwise he gets home first and has to watch himself."

David Michael is my six-year-old brother.

My big brothers, Charlie and Sam, and I are each responsible for him one afternoon a week until Mom gets home from work. Kathy, this fifteen-year-old girl who lives a few blocks from us, watches him the other two afternoons. Kathy gets paid to watch him. Charlie and Sam and I don't.

Mary Anne and I ran all the way home. We reached my front yard, sweaty and out of breath. And there was David Michael, sitting forlornly on the front steps, his dark curls falling limply across his forehead.

He burst into tears as soon as he saw us.

"What's wrong?" I asked. I sat down beside him and put my arm around his shoulders.

"I'm locked out," he wailed.

"What happened to your key?"

David Michael shook his head. "I don't know." He wiped his eyes, hiccuping.

"Well," I said, "it's all right." I got my own key out of my purse.

David Michael burst into fresh tears. "No, it's not! It's not all right. I couldn't get in and I have to go to the bathroom."

I unlocked the door. When David Michael gets like this, it's best just to sort of ignore his tears and pretend everything is fine.

Mary Anne and I held the door open for him and I ushered him into the bathroom. Our collie Louie tore outside as we went in. He was frantic to get outdoors after being locked in the house since breakfast time.

"While you go to the bathroom," I told David Michael, "I'm going to fix us some lemonade, okay?"

David Michael actually smiled. "Okay!"

I'm good with children. So is Mary Anne. Mom says so. Both of us get lots of afternoon and weekend baby-sitting jobs. In fact, I'd been offered a job for that afternoon, but I had to turn it down because of David Michael.

That reminded me. "Hey," I said to Mary Anne as I turned on the air conditioning, "Mrs. Newton asked me to baby-sit for Jamie this afternoon. Didn't she call you after she called me?"

Mary Anne sat down at the kitchen table and watched me put lemonade mix in a big glass pitcher. She shook her head. "No. Maybe she called Claudia."

Claudia Kishi lives across the street from me. She and Mary Anne and I have lived on Bradford Court since we were born. We've grown up together, but somehow Claudia has never spent as much time with us as Mary Anne and I have spent with each other. For one thing, Claudia's really into art and always off at art classes, or else holed up in her room painting or drawing. Or reading mysteries. That's her other passion. She's much more grown-up than Mary Anne and I. When we were little, Mary Anne and I were always playing school or dolls or dress-up, but we practically had to brainwash Claudia to get her to join us. A lot of the time, we just didn't bother, but Claud's always been good for a bike ride or going to the movies or the community pool. As far as I'm concerned, one of the best things about Claudia is that her father isn't Mr. Spier. Mr. Kishi can be strict about Claudia's schoolwork, but he doesn't faint if you suggest going downtown for a Coke or something.

Still, Claudia has never been a close friend, and this year, the gap between us seems to have widened just since school started. Even though we're all seventh-graders, Claudia suddenly seemed . . . older. She talks about boys, and spends most of her time adding to her wardrobe and talking on the phone. In the short time since school started, she's become a different person.

David Michael came into the kitchen looking much cheerier.

"Here you go," I said. I handed him a glass of lemonade as he sat next to Mary Anne.

Charlie came in then, tossing a football

around. Sam got home a few minutes later, with our collie Louie skidding along behind him. Charlie is sixteen and Sam is fourteen. They both go to Stoneybrook High. Sam's a freshman this year, and Charlie's a junior.

"Hi, everybody. Hi, squirt," Charlie said to David Michael.

"I am not a squirt," replied David Michael.

Charlie thought he was so great because he'd just made the varsity team. You'd think he was the first person ever to play football for Stoneybrook High.

"We're going to play ball in the Hansons' backyard," Sam announced. "Want to play, Kristy?"

I did, but David Michael wouldn't want to. He was too little. "I don't know. I thought Mary Anne and I would take David Michael to the brook. You want to go wading, David Michael?" I asked.

He nodded happily.

"See you guys later," I called as Sam and Charlie left the house, slamming the front door behind them.

Mary Anne and I took David Michael and Louie to the brook. We watched David Michael wade and make sailboats and try to catch minnows. Louie ran around, looking for squirrels.

"I'd better go," Mary Anne said after an hour or so. "Dad will be home soon."

"Yeah. Mom will be home soon, too. David Michael," I called, "time to leave."

He stood up reluctantly and the three of us and Louie walked home together.

When we reached our driveway, David Michael ran across the lawn, and Mary Anne whispered to me, "Nine o'clock, okay?"

I grinned. "Okay." Mary Anne and I have a secret code. Mary Anne made it up. We can signal each other with flashlights. If I look out my bedroom window I can see right into hers. Lots of nights we talk to each other with the flashlights, since Mary Anne isn't allowed on the phone after dinner except for things like baby-sitting jobs or getting homework assignments.

When Mom came home a little while later, she had a pizza with her. My brothers and I stood around the kitchen breathing in the smell of cheese and pepperoni.

But Sam and Charlie looked skeptical. "I wonder what she wants," murmured Sam.

"Yeah," said Charlie.

Mom only gets pizza when she has to ask us a favor.

I decided not to beat around the bush. "How come you bought a pizza, Mom?" I asked.

Charlie kicked my ankle, but I ignored him. "Come on. What do you have to ask us?"

Mom grinned. She knew exactly what she was doing. And she knew that we knew it. "Oh, all right," she said. "Kathy called me at work to say she won't be able to watch David Michael tomorrow. I was wondering what you guys are — "

"Football practice," said Charlie promptly.

"Math Club," said Sam.

"Sitting at the Newtons'," I said.

"Drat," said Mom.

"But we *are* sorry," added Sam.

"I know you are."

Then we dug into the pizza while Mom started making phone calls.

She called Mary Anne. Mary Anne was sitting for the Pikes.

She called Claudia. Claudia had an art class.

She called two high school girls. They had cheerleading practice.

David Michael looked like he might cry.

Finally Mom called Mrs. Newton and asked if she would mind if I brought David Michael with me when I sat for Jamie. Luckily, Mrs. Newton didn't mind.

I chewed away at a gloppy mouthful of cheese and pepperoni and thought it was too bad that Mom's pizza had to get cold while she made all those phone calls. I thought it was too bad that David Michael had to sit there and feel like he was causing a lot of trouble just because he was only six years old and couldn't take care of himself yet.

Then the idea for the Baby-sitters Club came to me and I almost choked.

I could barely wait until nine o'clock so I could signal the great idea to Mary Anne.

CHAPTER 2

After dinner that night I went to my bedroom and shut my door. Then I sat down at my desk with a pad of paper and a sharpened pencil. I had three things to do: the composition on decorum, my homework, and some thinking about the Baby-sitters Club. I planned to do them in that order, grossest first.

I looked up *decorum* in my dictionary. It said: "Conformity to social convention; propriety. See Synonyms at *etiquette*." I had to look up both *propriety* and *etiquette* before I got the picture. Then I understood. I'd been rude. Why hadn't Mr. Redmont just said so? It would have made things a lot simpler. So I wrote down some stuff about how being rude was distracting to other students and made Stoneybrook Middle School look bad to visitors. I counted the words. Ninety-eight. So I added

"The End" with a great big flourish, and hoped for the best.

Then I did the math assignment and read about Paraguay for social studies.

And *then* it was time to think about the Baby-sitters Club.

I smoothed out a fresh piece of paper and started making a list:

> 1. *Members:*
>   *Me*
>   *Mary Anne*
>   *Claudia*
>   *Who else?*
>
> 2. *Advertising:*
>   *Fliers*
>   *Telephone*
>   *Newspaper?*
>
> 3. *Set up meeting times when clients*
>   *can call to line up sitters.*
>   *Where to meet?*
>
> 4. *Weekly dues for expenses?*

My idea was that Mary Anne and Claudia and I would form a club to do baby-sitting. We would tell people (our clients) that at certain times during the week we could all be reached at one number. We would hold our meetings during those times. That way when someone needed a sitter, he or she could make one phone call and reach three different people. One of us would be available for sure. Of course, people could call us individually at other times, but the beauty of the meetings would be the opportunity to reach several baby-sitters at once. That way, our clients wouldn't have to go through what Mom had just gone through at dinner.

We would have to advertise ourselves, I decided. I was hoping Claudia would help us make up some fliers to stick in the mailboxes in our neighborhood. She'd be able to draw something really cute on our ads.

I looked at my watch. It was a quarter to nine. Fifteen more minutes before I was supposed to signal Mary Anne. I was getting edgy. I had such a terrific idea and I couldn't even pick up the phone like a normal human being to tell Mary Anne about it. Mr. Spier would just tell me I could see Mary Anne in school tomorrow.

I sighed.

Mom knocked on my door. I knew it was Mom because none of my brothers ever bothers to knock. They just barge in.

"Come in," I called.

"Hi, sweetie," said Mom. She closed the door behind her and sat on the edge of my bed. "How was school?"

Mom tries to spend a little time alone with each of us kids every day. She feels guilty that she and my father are divorced and that she has to work full-time to support us. She's told us so. I wish she wouldn't feel guilty. It's not her fault that Dad ran off to California and got married again and doesn't send Mom much child support money. Mom says she doesn't want more money, though. She has a terrific job at this big company in Stamford, and she likes the fact that she can support us so well. It makes her feel proud and independent. But she still feels guilty.

My father can be sort of a jerk sometimes. He hasn't called us in over a year. And he even forgot my twelfth birthday last month.

I paused, trying to think of a way to answer Mom's question without telling her about the composition I'd had to write.

"Kristy?" Mom asked.

"It was fine."

"Okay, what happened?"

There is absolutely no fooling Mom.

"Well," I said, "you know how hot it was today?"

"Yes."

"And you know how sometimes a hot day can seem really long?"

"Kristy, get to the point."

So I did. And Mom laughed. Then she read my composition and said she thought it was fine. I asked her if she thought "The End" could count as the ninety-ninth and one-hundredth words, and she smiled and said she hoped so.

My mom is really great.

When she left to go talk to Sam, it was nine o'clock.

I got out my flashlight, turned off the lamp by my desk, and stood at the window that faced Mary Anne's room.

I flashed the light once to let her know I was there.

She flashed back. Good, she was ready.

Then I flashed out this message (it took forever):

HAVE GREAT IDEA FOR BABY-SITTERS CLUB. MUST TALK. IMPORTANT. CAN'T WAIT. WE CAN GET LOTS OF JOBS.

There was a pause. Then Mary Anne flashed: WHAT? and I had to start all over again. I shortened the message. At last Mary Anne flashed: TERRIFIC. SEE YOU TOMORROW. And we put the flashlights away. Mary Anne hasn't been caught once and we plan to keep it that way.

I was just closing the drawer where I hide my flashlight, when Mom knocked again.

"Come in," I said curiously, turning the light on. Mom doesn't usually come back for a second chat. On the other hand, I don't usually keep my door closed for so long.

This time, Mom sat at my desk and I sat on the bed.

"I just wanted to let you know," she said, "that I'm going out with Watson on Saturday night. I forgot to tell you before."

I groaned. Mom has been seeing this guy, Watson, off and on for about four months. She likes him a lot, but I don't like him much at all. He's divorced from his wife and has two little kids. Plus, he's getting bald.

"I'm not asking for your permission, Kristy," Mom said. "I just want you to be able to plan on my being out Saturday. Charlie's got a date, but Sam will be home."

I nodded.

"I wish you could be a little more open-minded about Watson," said Mom. "I can't make you like him, but you haven't given him much of a chance."

The truth is, I haven't given any of the men Mom has dated a chance. I'm afraid that if I break down and treat them nicely, one of them might marry Mom. Think what could happen then. We're happy the way we are.

"One more thing," said Mom. "This is Watson's weekend to have the children and he has to work on Saturday morning. He doesn't like it, but that's the way it is. He wondered if you'd baby-sit for Andrew and Karen while he's at the office."

I shook my head. Watson has asked me at least three times to sit for his kids, but I won't do it. I don't want to have anything to do with him or his family. I either make up an excuse or else I flatly refuse.

"Okay," said Mom. "It's your choice." She sounded as if she meant, It's your funeral.

But she came over to me and kissed the top of my head, so I knew she wasn't angry.

"Going to bed soon?" she asked.

"Yeah. You can leave the door open," I told her as she left my room.

I said good-night to my brothers, and a half hour later I crawled into bed. Louie sacked out next to me. I lay there stroking him and thinking about Mom and Watson and Andrew and Karen. Then I remembered the Baby-sitters Club and cheered up.

Tomorrow couldn't come fast enough!

CHAPTER 3

Mr. Redmont accepted my composition on decorum. I handed it to him before school, so he wouldn't have to read it while the entire class was hanging around. He didn't count the words, just skimmed it, looked up at me, and said, "This is fine, Kristy. Fine work. You express yourself very nicely on paper."

And that was it. No words of wisdom, no scolding.

I heaved a sigh of relief and walked to my desk with decorum.

After school, Mary Anne and I ran home together again. It wasn't quite as hot as it had been the day before, so we weren't as uncomfortable.

"You're sitting for the Pikes today?" I asked Mary Anne as we jogged along.

Mary Anne nodded.

"How many of them?" There are eight Pike children.

"Two. Claire and Margo."

"Oh, not bad," I said. Claire and Margo are four and six. They're fun. More importantly, they like baby-sitters.

"Where are you sitting today?" asked Mary Anne.

"The Newtons'. David Michael is coming with me. He can play with Jamie."

"Oh, hey, great! Maybe I'll bring Claire and Margo over for a while. They can all play together. And then you can tell me about the baby-sitting club."

"Okay!" I agreed.

We parted when we reached my house, and I was glad to see that I'd gotten home before David Michael. I let Louie out and made a pitcher of lemonade.

At 3:30 sharp, David Michael and I were standing on the Newtons' front steps. Punctuality is an important part of baby-sitting. I have never once been late for a job. My customers appreciate that.

I let David Michael ring the bell. In a few seconds the front door was flung wide open.

"Hi-hi!" exclaimed Jamie. Jamie is three.

David Michael gave me a look that said, I

have to play with a three-year-old who goes *hi-hi*?

I patted David Michael on the back.

"Hi, Jamie," I replied.

"Look!" he exclaimed, as we stepped into the Newtons' front hall. "Look what I got!" He held out a little doll in an army uniform. "It's a G.I. Joe."

"Really?" said David Michael, suddenly interested.

"Yup," said Jamie proudly.

"Got any others?" asked my little brother.

"Sure," replied Jamie. "Come on."

The boys ran off. Mrs. Newton greeted me from the kitchen. "Thank goodness for G.I. Joe," she said.

I smiled. "Sorry about David Michael, but it looks like it'll work out okay." I never like to impose on my clients.

"I'm sure it will be fine." Mrs. Newton patted her bulging stomach. "Jamie better get used to other children."

"How long until the baby's due?" I asked.

"About eight weeks."

I sighed. "Oh, I wish it would hurry up!"

"*You* wish!"

Mrs. Newton gave me the instructions for the afternoon. "Just the doctor's appointment and a few errands," she reminded me. "I should be back by five-thirty."

"Okay. Five-thirty," I repeated.

As soon as she was gone, I called Mary Anne at the Pikes'. "Come over whenever you want to," I said.

The Pikes live just a few doors away, so Mary Anne showed up in ten minutes. She was pulling Claire and Margo in a red wagon.

"Hi-hi!" Jamie greeted them cheerfully.

"Hi-hi!" Claire, the four-year-old, replied.

David Michael and Margo eyed each other suspiciously. They hadn't played together much, and David Michael was wary of any little girl, especially one who wasn't in his class at school.

We took the kids out back to Jamie's swings. When they were playing happily, Mary Anne said, "So what about the baby-sitting club?"

"Well," I replied, "I thought we could get together with a couple of other girls who baby-sit and form a club — sort of like a company — "

We were interrupted by a thump and a wail.

Jamie had fallen off one of the swings.

"*Wahhh!*" he cried.

I ran to him and checked him over. No bumps, no skinned knees.

"*Wahh!*"

"Where does it hurt?" I asked him.

He pointed to his tummy, then let his hand

drift to his knee, and finally up to his head.

"Everywhere?" I suggested.

He nodded miserably.

"Maybe we better go," said Mary Anne, rounding up Claire and Margo.

"Okay," I replied. "Listen, why don't we tell Claudia the idea? Let's go over to her house when we're done sitting. She'll be back from her art class then."

"Okay. See you."

Inside, I gave Jamie a cookie, and he and David Michael played with the G.I. Joes and then watched *Sesame Street* on TV. Jamie's accident was long forgotten by the time his mother came home.

Mrs. Newton paid me and I ran to my house, leaving David Michael with Sam, and then ran across the street to Claudia Kishi's.

Recently, I haven't felt quite as comfortable visiting Claudia as I used to. This year she had to go and start growing up faster than us. She's wearing a bra, and the way she talks, you'd think boys had just been invented.

She acts like all the guys in the seventh grade aren't the same goony boys they were last year. Last year, the boys were saying, "Want some ABC gum?" and then handing us the gum out of their mouths, saying, "It's Already-Been-Chewed, get it?" and laughing

24

hysterically. Last year, the boys were giving us noogies on our arms and throwing spitballs at us. Last year, the boys were pulling our chairs out from under us when we stood up to answer questions. *This* year (if you listen to Claudia), the boys are heroes. Personally, I don't see any change.

I rang the Kishis' bell. Claudia came to the door. She was wearing short, very baggy lavender plaid overalls, a white lacy blouse, a black fedora, and red high-top sneakers without socks. Her long black hair was carefully arranged in four braids. I felt extremely blah compared to her.

I was so used to seeing Claudia in outfits like that that I didn't bat an eye. What I did notice was that she was wearing makeup. There was blue stuff on her eyelids, gold stuff above her eyes, and magenta stuff on her cheeks.

"Claudia!" I gasped. "Your face! You look like" — I couldn't stop myself in time — "you got made up for the circus. . . . I mean . . . it's so *colorful*. . . ."

"Thanks a lot."

"No, honestly, Claud. You don't *need* makeup. You've got such a beautiful face. . . ."

"Oh, you just think it's exotic," said Claudia.

Well, maybe I do. Claudia's parents are

originally from Japan. They came to the United States when they were very young. Claudia has silky, jet-black hair, dark eyes, and creamy skin without so much as a trace of a pimple. She's absolutely gorgeous. But she has this wild streak in her that makes her buy belts made of feathers and wear knee socks with palm trees on them. Makeup was something new, though.

"Are you going to wear *that*" — I pointed to her face — "to school tomorrow?"

"If I can get away with it."

I nodded. Claudia's parents are very conservative. They don't understand her taste in clothes at all. They're pretty nice about the fedoras and stuff, although they won't buy any of those things for her. (That's why she has to baby-sit — to earn money for all that stuff.) But I didn't know how the Kishis would react to Claudia's day-glo face. I didn't know how our teachers would react, either.

I said hello to Mimi, Claudia's grandmother, who was busy making dinner, and followed Claudia upstairs to her room. "Where's Janine?" I asked.

Claudia rolled her eyes. "At the university, where else?"

Janine is Claudia's fifteen-year-old sister. She's only a sophomore in high school, but she's taking classes at Stoneybrook University. This is because Janine is a real live genius. An average person has an IQ of 100. An above average person has an IQ of 120 to 140. A person with an IQ of 150 is considered a genius.

Janine's IQ is 196.

Sometimes she makes me want to barf. She almost always makes Claudia want to barf. She thinks she knows everything. (Actually, she does.) She's forever correcting us. If I say, "David Michael, you can't play outside today because it's raining," Janine will say, "Kristy, you should say, 'David Michael, you *may not* play outside today.' If you say he *can't*, it means he's physically unable to, and that's not true. What you mean is that he does not have *permission* to play out of doors."

Janine sounds like a textbook. Her best friend is this fourteen-year-old math nerd who's going to graduate from high school in the spring. Her second best friend is her computer.

I'm sure it's because of Janine that Claudia concentrates on art and is a terrible student.

I was relieved to hear that Janine wasn't home.

Claudia and I plopped down on her bed. "Mary Anne'll be here in a few minutes," I said. "I have this really great idea that I want to tell both of you about."

Claudia's eyes lit up. "What is it?"

"A baby-sitters club," I announced.

"A baby-sitters club?" she squealed.

"Yeah, I'll explain it all when — " Just then, the doorbell rang.

Claudia thundered down the stairs, yelling, "I'll get it!" She flung open the front door and hauled Mary Anne up to her room. "I like clubs!" she exclaimed. "Tell us your idea!"

"Well, it all started last night," I began. I told them how Mom had had to call nearly everyone in Stoneybrook, looking for a baby-sitter, and how long it had taken, and how bad David Michael had felt. "So I thought we could sort of join together. We all baby-sit anyway. We could advertise ourselves and get more customers. We should meet a few times each week and tell our customers what those times are. Then they can make one call and reach a whole bunch of us at once. And if, like, Mrs. Pike wants *two* sitters, she'll only have to make one call." I explained everything else I had thought of, and wound up with, "Okay, here are two things to think about: One, where should we hold our meetings; and two, who else could we ask to join the club?"

"I can answer both questions," said Claudia. "We should hold the meetings here, because I have a phone in my room."

"Oh, terrific!" I exclaimed. (I'd been hoping Claudia would suggest that.)

"And I know someone who might want to join the club."

"Who?" Mary Anne and I asked.

"She's new. She just moved to Stoneybrook. She lives right over on Fawcett Avenue, and she's in my class. Her name is Stacey McGill."

"Well, okay . . ." I said slowly. "Of course, we'll have to meet her."

"Oh, sure. You'll really like her. She's from New York City," Claudia added.

I was impressed. I could tell Mary Anne was, too. She opened her eyes wide. "I wonder why her family wanted to leave *there* to come *here*," she said.

Claudia shrugged. "Don't know. But I'm glad they did. Stacey's really cool."

Mary Anne and I glanced at each other, not sure that this was a good sign.

"What's everyone doing tomorrow afternoon?" asked Claudia. "Can we meet then?"

"If it's at five-thirty again," said Mary Anne. "I have to baby-sit before then."

We agreed to meet late the next afternoon. And that was how the Baby-sitters Club officially began.

CHAPTER 4

Promptly at 5:30 the next afternoon, I crossed the street to Claudia's house and rang the bell. Claudia answered it again, this time wearing a baggy yellow- and black-checked shirt, black pants, red jazz shoes, and a bracelet that looked like it was made from a telephone cord. Her earrings were dangling jointed skeletons that jumped around when she moved. I noticed she wasn't wearing any makeup.

"Mom and Dad wouldn't let me," she said.

"Well, you got away with the skeletons."

Claudia grinned. "I didn't put those on until I got to school," she whispered. "Mimi's the only grown-up home now and she doesn't mind if I wear skeletons."

"Oh, very sneaky!" Claudia knows every trick.

As we went up the stairs, Claudia said,

"Stacey's already here. I really hope you like her." She lowered her voice. "And Janine's home."

I groaned.

"Sorry. Her door's open, too."

At that moment, Janine stuck her head out into the hall. "Oh, hi, Kristy," she said. "I thought I heard voices. Claudia told me about the Baby-sitters Club. That sounds like an outstanding idea."

"Well, hopefully it will — " I began.

Janine's face took on her know-it-all look. "Kristy, *hopefully* is one of the most commonly misused words in the English language. The word means 'in a hopeful manner.' It is not acceptable to use it to mean 'it is to be hoped.' If I were — "

I didn't have the vaguest idea what she was talking about. "Gee, Janine, I gotta go," I cut her off as Claudia went on into her room. "Stacey's waiting for us. See you." I really cannot take much of Janine. And I *always* make a mistake in front of her. I don't know how Claudia manages to live in the same house with her.

Just as I reached Claudia's bedroom, the doorbell rang. "That's Mary Anne," I called. "I'll let her in, Claud." I ran downstairs, opened the door, warned Mary Anne about

Janine, then ran back upstairs with Mary Anne at my heels. We ran straight to Claudia's room, careful not to look in at Janine as we ran by her open door.

"Hi," Claudia said, closing her door behind us. "You guys, this is Stacey McGill. Stacey, this is Kristy Thomas and this is Mary Anne Spier."

"Hi!" Stacey and I said brightly.

Mary Anne suddenly turned shy. "Hi," she said softly, speaking more to a wall than to Stacey.

I looked at Stacey. I could see why she and Claudia were friends already. Stacey had on a pink sweat shirt with sequins and a large purple parrot on the front; short, tight-fitting jeans with zippers up the outsides of the legs; and pink plastic shoes. She was very pretty, tall and quite thin with huge blue eyes framed by dark lashes, and fluffy blonde hair that looked as if it had been permed recently. I glanced at Mary Anne. She and I were still in our school clothes — skirts and blouses. I was wearing white knee socks and loafers. Mary Anne was wearing short white socks and saddle shoes. Mary Anne's hair was, of course, in braids, and I was wearing a blue hair band.

We looked like second-graders. Stacey and Claudia looked like models.

There was an uncomfortable silence.

"Well," I cleared my throat. "Claudia, did you tell Stacey about the Baby-sitters Club?"

"Just what we talked about yesterday," she replied.

"Did you baby-sit in New York?" I asked Stacey.

"Oh, all the time. We lived in this big building. There were over two hundred apartments in it — "

"Wow," said Mary Anne.

" — and I used to put up signs in the laundry room. People called me all the time." She paused. "I can stay out until ten on Friday and Saturday nights."

Another "Wow" from Mary Anne.

I was feeling more and more like a baby. How was it possible to feel so much younger than someone who was the same age as you?

"I'd really like to be in the club," said Stacey. "I don't know too many kids in Stoneybrook yet. And it'd be nice to earn some money. My mom and dad buy my clothes, but I have to earn money for other things — you know, tapes and jewelry and stuff."

"How come you left New York?" asked Mary Anne. Mary Anne has a real thing for New York — for glamour and lights and stores. She wants to live in the city after she's grown up.

Stacey looked at the floor. She started jiggling her right foot back and forth. "Oh," she said lightly, "my dad changed his job. Gosh, you have a lot of neat posters, Claudia."

"Thanks. I made those two myself." Claudia pointed to a picture of a horse galloping through a desert, and to another of a girl sitting on a window seat, gazing outside.

"Boy, if I lived in New York I wouldn't leave for anything," Mary Anne went on. "Tell me what it's like to live there. What was your school like?"

"Well," began Stacey, "I went to a private school."

"Did you have to wear a uniform?" asked Claudia, shuddering.

"Nope. We could wear regular clothes."

"How did you get to school?" asked Mary Anne.

"On the subway."

"Wow."

"Once," Stacey added, seeing how impressed Mary Anne was, "I took the subway all the way from our apartment to Coney Island. I had to change about a zillion times."

"Wow. Did you ever take a cab by yourself?"

"Sure. Lots of times."

"Wow."

At Mary Anne's last "Wow" we all began giggling.

"Well, anyway," I said, "to get back to the Baby-sitters Club, what I think we should do is make two lists: one of rules, and one of things to do — "

"Does this mean," Stacey interrupted me, "that I'm in the club?"

I glanced at Mary Anne, who nodded her head. I already knew what Claudia thought.

"Yup," I said.

"Oh, hey! Great!" Stacey exclaimed, grinning.

Claudia gave her the thumbs-up sign. Then she pulled a package of peanut M&M's from under her pillow. "We should celebrate," she said, handing the candy around.

Mary Anne and I were starved and each gobbled down a handful, but Stacey just glanced in the package and then passed it back to Claudia. "These are — you've only got five left," she said.

"Oh, go ahead," replied Claudia. "I've got lots of stuff stashed away. Mom and Dad don't know about it." She said she had bubble gum in her underwear drawer, a chocolate bar behind her encyclopedias, a package of Twinkies in her desk drawer, and some Wint-o-green Lifesavers in her piggy bank.

"No, thanks," said Stacey. "I'm, um, on a diet."

"You?" I cried. "You're skinny already!" Stacey was the first person my age I knew who was on a diet. "How much do you weigh?" I demanded.

"Kristy!" Claudia exclaimed. "That's none of your business."

"But it's not safe to diet if you don't need to. My mom said. Does your mother know you're dieting?"

"Well, she — "

"See, I'll bet she doesn't."

At that moment, someone knocked on Claudia's door. "Mary Anne!" Janine called. "Your father phoned on the other line. He says it's time for you to go home."

Mary Anne looked at her watch. "Six-ten!" she cried. "Oh, no, I'm late. Dad hates it when I'm late. Thanks, Janine. I have to go, you guys."

"Wait," I said. "We didn't finish making our plans."

"Let's meet tomorrow at recess," suggested Claudia.

"Really?" I said. Recently, Claudia has been spending recess watching the cute boys play basketball. She never wants to play four-square or tetherball with Mary Anne and me.

"Sure," she said. "As soon as we're done with lunch we'll meet outside by the gym door. Somebody remember to bring a pad of paper and a pen."

"I will," I volunteered.

Mary Anne stood up then and practically flew home.

"I better go, too," said Stacey.

"Me, too," I said.

Claudia walked us to the door and we went our separate ways.

The Friday lunch at Stoneybrook Middle School is always the same: sloppy joes, red Jell-O with canned fruit in it, a dinky cup of coleslaw, milk, and a fudgesicle.

I truly hate it, except for the fudgesicle.

After Mary Anne and I had forced down as much as possible, we went outside to wait for Claudia and Stacey. We hadn't sat with them in the cafeteria because they were eating at a table full of the most sophisticated seventh-grade girls (whom we hardly knew) *and* some boys. How they could eat with boys was beyond me. The boys are always doing gross things like smushing up peas and ravioli in their milk cartons to see what colors they can make. Claudia seems to think those things are hilarious.

So Mary Anne and I reached the gym door first. We played a fast game of tetherball while we waited. I won. I usually do. I'm good at sports.

"Hi, you guys!" called Claudia about ten minutes later. She and Stacey were walking across the playground.

"Hi!" we answered.

The four of us went to a quiet corner of the school building and sat down on some empty packing crates.

"I've got the paper and pen," I said. "And something else." I pulled the list that I had made Tuesday night from my pocket and pointed to section two, which was labeled ADVERTISING. "This is what we have to do next: Let people know what we're doing."

"Right," agreed Claudia from underneath an outrageous red felt hat, which her teacher wouldn't allow her to wear in the classroom.

"I think fliers are the easiest way to tell people about our club. We can make up a nice ad and my mom can Xerox it at her office. Then we can stick copies in people's mailboxes. We can do it in our neighborhood and on other streets, too. Anywhere that's in bike-riding distance. Mary Anne, your dad would let you sit in another neighborhood if it weren't *too* far way, wouldn't he?"

"I guess so," Mary Anne replied uncertainly.

I saw Stacey glance curiously at Mary Anne.

"Good," I said. "Now, we already have a name — the Baby-sitters Club. Do you think we should have some kind of symbol or sign, too? You know, like the symbol that's on Girl Scout cookies, or the sun that's on the stationery my mom's company uses?"

"Yeah!" said Stacey. "That's a good idea. We could put it on top of our fliers. Claudia, you could draw something for us."

"I don't know," said Claudia.

"Come on, you're a great artist," I exclaimed. "You can draw anything."

"I know I can draw, but I'm not good at . . . at symbols and stuff. Janine's better at those things."

"Oh, forget Janine," I said. "Anyway, we're all going to think of the symbol. We're a club. We have to agree on things. Now what could we use?"

"Well," said Mary Anne, "it could either be something that has to do with baby-sitters, like a child or a helping hand, or it could just be something we like: a rainbow or a shooting star or a frog — "

"A frog!" I burst out. I began to giggle. So did Claudia and Stacey.

Mary Anne looked embarrassed. Then she began to laugh, too.

"How about a warthog?" suggested Claudia.

"A nerd!" said Stacey.

"Dog food!" We were all laughing so hard we could barely talk.

"Okay, let's be serious," I said when we had calmed down. "Lunch is going to be over in ten minutes."

"How about something with our names in it?" suggested Stacey.

"Yeah!" said Mary Anne and Claudia and I, but then we couldn't think of anything.

"How about an alphabet block with our initials on it?" said Mary Anne.

"That's cute," said Claudia, "but there are four of us, and you can't show more than three sides of a block at one time."

"Oh . . . yeah," said Mary Anne slowly. Claudia understands that kind of thing better than we do.

"Wait a minute!" Claudia cried. "I've got it. I could draw something like this." She took the pen and paper from me and drew this:

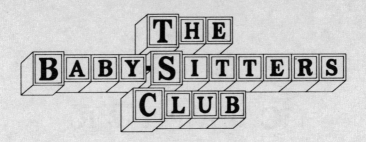

THE
BABY-SITTERS
CLUB

"That's terrific! Really terrific!" I exclaimed. "It's perfect! Claudia, you're a — " I stopped. I'd almost said genuis, but Claudia's pretty touchy about that word. " — a pro," I finished.

The bell rang then and we had to go inside. But first we agreed to spend the weekend working on the Baby-sitters Club.

CHAPTER 5

On Saturday the four members of the Baby-sitters Club worked very hard. Mary Anne and Claudia and I called all the families we already baby-sat for and told them about the club. Then we wrote up a little ad about the club and phoned it into the *Stoneybrook News*. It would appear on Wednesday. We couldn't wait to see it.

Then Stacey had an idea. "I think we should elect, you know, officers of the club." We were sitting around in Claudia's room as usual.

"Officers?" Claudia repeated, looking confused. She was probably thinking of policemen.

"Yeah. A president, a vice-president, a secretary, and . . . and. . . ."

"A treasurer!" I supplied. "Perfect. Four officers, four of us."

42

"Oh, I get it," said Claudia. "Well, I nominate Kristy for president. The club was her idea."

"I second it," said Mary Anne.

"Me, too," said Stacey. "It's unanimous."

I grinned. "Wow! Thanks, you guys. Okay, I nominate Claudia for vice-president since we're using her room and her phone and phone number. She may get a lot of calls to handle when the rest of us aren't here."

"I second it," said Mary Anne.

"Me, too," chimed in Stacey. "Unanimous again."

Claudia beamed.

Mary Anne cleared her throat and looked around nervously. "Stacey, if you don't mind, I'd like to be secretary. I'm good at writing things down."

"That's perfect," said Stacey, "because I'm good with money and numbers. I was hoping I could be treasurer."

We didn't even bother to vote on Mary Anne and Stacey since everything was working out so well.

In celebration of the new officers, Claudia took a bag of Gummy Bears out of her pencil case and passed it around.

Before the bag even reached Stacey, she

leaped up, clapped her hands over her mouth, and exclaimed, "Oh, no! I have to go home, but I'll be right back."

"Stacey," I said, "if you're still on that dumb diet, you can just say so. You don't have to run away. Look, we'll put the Gummy Bears back."

"No, no, it's not that. I just — I just forgot something. It'll only take a minute." Stacey dashed out of Claudia's room.

Mary Anne and Claudia and I looked at each other and shrugged.

Stacey returned about twenty minutes later. Her hands were empty.

"Where is it?" I asked her.

"Where's what?"

"What you forgot."

"What I . . . ? Oh, no, I just forgot to *do* something. But it's all taken care of."

I started to ask her another question, but Claudia flashed me a look that said I was being a pest.

We worked on our flier then, and when it was all finished, this is what it looked like:

Need a baby-sitter?
Save time! Call:

THE BABY-SITTERS CLUB
KL 5-3231

Monday, Wednesday, Friday 5:30–6:00
and reach four experienced baby-sitters.

Kristy Thomas, President
Claudia Kishi, Vice-President
Mary Anne Spier, Secretary
Stacey McGill, Treasurer

Available:
weekends
after school
evenings

Or call us one at a time, any time:

Kristy Thomas	*KL 5-4378*
Claudia Kishi	*KL 5-3231*
Mary Anne Spier	*KL 5-9102*
Stacey McGill	*KL 5-7844*

"I'll give the flier to my mom," I said. "She can Xerox it on Monday and we can pass around the fliers next week. I've got to go home anyway. It's almost dinnertime, and Mom's going out with Watson tonight." I made a face.

"Who's Watson?" asked Stacey.

"Her boyfriend," I replied. "My parents are divorced."

"Oh," said Stacey, looking slightly uncomfortable.

"Are your parents divorced, too?" I asked. I realized how little I knew about her.

"Nope. They've been married for fifteen years."

"Mine have been married for twenty years," said Claudia.

"My mother died when I was a baby," said Mary Anne quietly. "She had cancer."

Again Stacey looked embarrassed.

"It's all right. Really. I don't remember her. But sometimes I wish I did."

I stood up. "Well, I really better go. See you guys tomorrow," I called as I started down the Kishis' stairs.

Watson arrived at 6:30.

David Michael ran to meet him. He loves Watson. That's because he doesn't remember

Dad, so he thinks Watson is better than no father at all.

I stayed in my room until Mom yelled up to me, "Kristy! Watson's here!"

Why does she always make me come down to see Watson? She knows how I feel about him.

"Coming," I said, trying to sound put-out, as if she had interrupted something important.

When I came downstairs, Watson was standing in the kitchen with cartons of Chinese food. "Surprise!" he said.

"What?" I asked suspiciously.

"Isn't this nice, Kristy?" said Mom brightly. "Watson brought over Chinese food so we can all eat together before he and I go out."

Watson's always bringing over food. You'd think he owned a restaurant.

"Who's taking care of your kids?" I asked pointedly. I thought it was really stinky that on the weekend his kids came to stay, Watson not only had to go to work, but left the kids with a baby-sitter while he went out with my mother.

"I found a very nice baby-sitter," Watson replied pleasantly. "She took care of Andrew and Karen this morning while I went to the office, and they liked her very much."

"Oh," I said.

Watson set the white cartons on the table and began opening them while Sam and I got out plates, napkins, and silverware. I made a face at Sam to show him what I thought about the dinner, but Sam said, "Thanks, Watson. This is really great." Sam and Charlie sort of like Watson, too. Once Sam even baby-sat for Watson's kids. I, for one, will never, ever baby-sit for them. I bet they're brats.

"Yeah," said Charlie. "I'm taking Carole out for hamburgers tonight, but I don't mind eating first." Charlie has a stomach like a trash compacter.

"Mom?" I asked. "Is there any of that leftover chili?"

Mom glared at me. She didn't answer my question.

"What's wrong, Kristy?" said Watson. "I thought you liked Chinese food."

"It's okay, I guess. But I don't feel like it tonight."

Watson looked slightly hurt.

When the table was set, we sat down and everyone began helping themselves to Moo Shoo pork and chicken with cashews and beef with snow peas and the other things Watson had brought. I was starving, and I *love* Chinese food, especially chicken with cashews, but I wouldn't let Watson know. Since there was no chili, I made myself a peanut butter and straw-berry jam sandwich. I slapped it on my plate and then began nibbling it into the shape of a snowman. I was just about to bite off the snowman's head when Watson said, "So, how are things, Kristy?"

"Fine."

"School okay?"

"Yup."

"What are you doing that's new or interest-ing?"

"Nothing."

"Hey, Watson, the Math Club won its third math meet yesterday," Sam said, coming to the rescue. He hates when I bug Watson.

Watson needed a second to collect himself. He doesn't understand me. "What, Sam? . . . Oh, your *third* meet? That's great!"

"And guess what!" exclaimed David Mi-chael. "Mom's going to get me a new G.I. Joe — one of the good guys."

"That sounds pretty exciting," said Watson. "I don't know much about G.I. Joe dolls, though. I don't think Andrew plays with them."

"Oh, he probably does," I said airily, "and you just don't know it because you're not around enough. All the boys play with them." I glanced at Mom. I could practically see smoke coming from her ears as she let me know that

49

I was getting into *trouble*, but I went on anyway. "Besides, they're action toys, not dolls. Right, David Michael?"

David Michael beamed. "Right, Kristy."

"And Karen probably has a Rainbow Brite doll. Ever heard of those?"

At that moment, Mom slammed her fork onto her plate. She stood up so fast she almost tipped her chair over. "Kristy, apologize to Watson this instant, and then go to your room."

"But," I said politely, "I haven't finished this delicious dinner yet."

"Kristin Amanda Thomas! You are *asking* for it, young lady!"

I got to my feet. "I'm sorry, Watson," I mumbled. I walked out of the kitchen and started up the stairs. When I was halfway up, I yelled over my shoulder, "I'm sorry you're such a terrible father!" Then I ran to my room and slammed the door.

See, the thing is, Watson is actually a very good father. Karen and Andrew and their mother live right here in Stoneybrook, and Watson has the kids at his house each time he's supposed to. Plus, he celebrates every other holiday with them, and never forgets the ones in-between. (My dad forgets holidays all the time.) But I still don't like Watson horning in on our family. He doesn't belong with us.

Mom and Watson left without saying good-bye to me.

I felt really guilty about what I'd done.

Before I went to sleep I left a note on Mom's bed. It said: *Dear Mom, I'm sorry I was so rude. I guess I haven't learned much about decorum yet. I hope you had fun on your date. I love you. Kristy.*

When I woke up the next morning, I found a note to me from Mom. It said: *Dear Kristy, I love you, too. Mom.*

CHAPTER 6

On Wednesday afternoon, I raced home from school and made a frantic search of the front yard for our copy of the *Stoneybrook News*. I found it under a peony bush in the garden. I threw my things on the ground, sat down right in the middle of the yard, and leafed through the paper until I found the advertising section. And sure enough, the fifth ad from the bottom in the third column was ours. This is what it looked like:

THE BABY-SITTERS CLUB

Need a baby-sitter?
Make one call, reach four sitters.
Call KL 5-3231 Mon., Wed., Fri., 5:30–6:00

We had wanted to include more information in the ad, like the other phone numbers, but when we called the newspaper, we found out they charged you per *line* to run an ad. Our little ad was already pretty expensive, and we'd had to use our entire first week's club dues to pay for it. Still, the ad was awfully exciting. It was fun being in the newspaper.

"Hey, Kristy, what are you doing?" Claudia came running across our lawn, her knapsack jouncing against her back.

"Look!" I exclaimed. "Here it is! Our ad!"

"Ooh, let me see!"

Claudia dropped to her knees beside me, and I jabbed at the ad.

"Wow! Now if we can just finish handing around those fliers today," she said, "we might actually get some calls on Friday."

"I know!" I felt like squealing and jumping up and down.

"Let's get Mary Anne to help us."

"Okay," I said. "And Stacey."

"No, she's busy this afternoon. She told me so in school today."

"What's she doing?"

"Don't know. Come on. Are you ready?"

"Let me just put my books inside," I said, "and see if Kathy got here yet. She's baby-sitting for David Michael today."

Kathy and David Michael were playing Candyland on the back porch, so I grabbed the last of the fliers from my desk and ran outside to Claudia. "My mom Xeroxed five more yesterday. That's all I have left," I said.

"I've got six more."

We found Mary Anne, who also had six left, and we took off on our bicycles for Quentin Court, which is a few streets away from Stacey's house. There we put the last of the fliers in mailboxes.

"Done!" I said to Claudia and Mary Anne.

They grinned at me.

"Now I guess we just sit back and wait for calls."

"Right."

"Right."

Two days later, the members of the Baby-sitters Club gathered eagerly in Claudia's bedroom. Even though the fliers said for clients to call us between 5:30 and 6:00, we all managed to show up early. I was the first person there. I knocked on Claudia's bedroom door, which now had an official-looking sign on it reading:

THE BABY-SITTERS CLUB
Hours: Mon., Wed., Fri. 5:30 — 6:00

"Come in!" called Claudia. It was only 4:30

when I entered her room, but I found her sitting cross-legged on the bed with the phone in her lap, one hand clutching the receiver.

"The phone's not going to run away, you know," I greeted her.

Claudia grinned sheepishly. "I know. I'm just so excited."

Actually, I was, too. "So am I!" I squealed suddenly. I dashed across the room and jumped on her bed. "I've been waiting all week for today to come. What do you think will happen? Oh, this has just got to work. I know we'll have some customers. We'll have customers, won't we?" I grabbed the phone from Claudia and held it in *my* lap.

A knock came at the door. It couldn't be a customer . . . could it?

Claudia and I glanced at each other.

"It's probably Mary Anne," I said.

"Oh, right," Claudia answered. "Come in!"

The door opened.

It was Janine.

My stomach dropped down around my knees.

Janine cleared her throat. "Ahem," she said. "I've been studying your sign from out here in the hall, and I'm wondering if possibly you've made a mistake."

I leaped up and ran over to the sign. I

couldn't see a thing wrong with it. *Baby-sitters* was spelled correctly; Claudia had remembered the double "T." She'd gotten all the abbreviations right, too.

I put my hands on my hips. *"What?"* I asked.

"Well," began Janine primly, "I'm not entirely sure that you *have* made a mistake. I'm trying to decide whether you need an apostrophe after the word *baby-sitters*. You see, without an apostrophe, the word is simply plural, meaning the club consisting of the several or many babysitters. The apostrophe after the "S" would make the word possessive, meaning the club *belonging* to the several or many baby-sitters. Now either way could be right, but I'm not sure whether — "

"Hello, everybody!" Stacey's voice rang up through the stairwell like the welcome sound of a boat's horn on a foggy night.

"Saved!" I said under my breath. "Hi, Stace!"

Stacey ran up the stairs and I spirited her into Claudia's bedroom and closed the door behind us, leaving Janine out in the hall puzzling over the Apostrophe Mystery.

Mary Anne arrived a few minutes later, luckily without running into Janine.

It was 5:05.

The four of us sat on Claudia's bed.

Nobody said a word.

At 5:10, Claudia got up, took a shoe box labeled SNEAKERS out of her closet, opened it, and handed around some jawbreakers. As usual, Stacey refused.

At 5:25, I began staring at my watch, following the minute hand around and around — 5:26, 5:27, 5:28, 5:29.

At exactly 5:30 the phone rang.

I screamed.

"Oh, no! I don't believe it!" cried Mary Anne.

Claudia spit out her jawbreaker. "I'll answer it, I'll answer it," she shrieked. She jerked up the receiver and said politely, "Good afternoon. Baby-sitters Club."

Then she made a face and handed me the phone. "Kristy, it's your mother."

I spit out my jawbreaker, too. "Mo-*om!*" I exclaimed as soon as I got on the phone. "These are our business hours. You're not supposed to — What? You do? Oh." I calmed down. "Please hold for a moment."

I put my hand over the receiver. "Mom needs a sitter for David Michael!" I cried. "Kathy can't come next Wednesday."

Everyone suppressed shrieks.

"I've got our appointment book right here," said Claudia. "Now let's see. Mary Anne, you have to go to the dentist that day, and I have art class. That leaves you" — Claudia pointed to me — "and Stacey."

What should we do? "Just another sec, Mom," I said.

I hadn't really thought about what to do if several of us were available for the same job.

"Well . . ." I began.

"He's your brother," Stacey said. "You should get the job."

"But if you took it, you'd get to know some other people in the neighborhood. You'd probably meet Sam and Charlie — they're my big brothers."

"Brothers?" Stacey's eyes lit up. Boys! "But what are you going to do while I baby-sit? Hang around and watch?"

"Well, I *hope* I'll have another job," I said huffily. "You take the job, Stacey. I don't want my first Baby-sitters Club client to be my own mother."

"Okay, if you're sure," Stacey said slowly. Then she grinned. "Thanks!"

"No problem," I said. I took my hand off of the receiver. "Mom, Stacey will baby-sit for David Michael on Wednesday. The usual time, right? . . . Okay. Hey, where are you calling from anyway? . . . Oh, the office."

Claudia elbowed me. "Quit tying up the line. Someone else might be trying to get through."

I nodded. "Mom, I have to get off. I'll see you in a little while. . . . Okay. . . . Okay. . . . Bye." I hung up.

The phone rang again immediately. Claudia gave me a look that said, I told you so.

"Can I answer it?" Mary Anne asked.

"Sure," I said.

Mary Anne picked up the phone. "Good afternoon. Baby-sitters Club," she said. There was a long pause. "I think you have the wrong number. There's no Jim Bartolini here." She hung up.

At 5:42 the phone rang for a third time. We all looked at each other. "You get it, Kristy," Mary Anne said. "You're the president."

"Okay. . . . Hello. Baby-sitters Club. . . . Yes . . . yes. Just a moment, please." I put my hand over the mouthpiece. "Do any of you know a Mrs. McKeever? She lives on Quentin Court."

The girls shook their heads.

"What's she got?" asked Claudia.

"Two kids, Buffy and Pinky," I replied.

"Buffy and Pinky!" cried Stacey. "*Buffy* and *Pinky?*"

"*Shhh,*" I warned her.

"How old are they?" Mary Anne wanted to know.

"I don't know. Hold on. . . . Hello, Mrs. McKeever? We need a little information, please. How old are Buffy and Pinky? . . . *Oh.* Okay." I turned back to the members of my club. "She says they're three. They must be twins."

"When does she need a sitter?" asked Mary Anne.

"Wednesday afternoon. Oh, I guess I'm the only one who's free then," I suddenly realized. I was dying for a new client anyway. I accepted the job and took down the information I needed. Then Mrs. McKeever asked me a zillion questions about myself. She wanted to know how old I was and how much experience I had and that sort of thing.

When I hung up the phone, I said to Mary Anne, "Hey, secretary, you've got to record these jobs in the appointment book."

"Oh, right." I handed her the book and she got right to work.

The next two calls were for Jim Bartolini.

Claudia was growing exasperated. "Boy, this is *weird*," she said. "I've gotten wrong numbers before, but no one's ever asked for Jim Bartolini. Certainly not three no ones."

At 5:55 Mary Anne stood up. "I better get going," she said. She pulled on her sweater and crunched loudly on the remaining bit of her jawbreaker.

The phone rang. Stacey answered it and handed it to me. "It's your mom again, Kristy."

I rolled my eyes. "Mom?" I said. "Did Kathy back out of her other afternoon, too? . . . Oh. . . . *Oh*. . . . *Oh*, no. Not *me*. I am *not* baby-sitting for them. You know how I feel. Okay, but hold on. . . . Watson needs a baby-sitter for his kids again on Saturday morning. Not tomorrow, but next Saturday," I told the others. *"I'm* not doing it."

"I'll do it," Mary Anne said. "I'm getting curious about them. Aren't you curious, Kristy?"

I was *dying* to see what kind of monsters Watson had. "Not really," I said. "Sign yourself up for the job."

As Mary Anne was about to walk out of Claudia's room, the phone rang for the seventh time since 5:30. "I'll get it," said Mary Anne. "One last call. . . . Hello? . . . *What?*" Mary Anne's braids practically stood on end. "It's some boy on the phone," she told us. "He says his name is Jim Bartolini. He wants to know if there have been any calls for him!"

"You're kidding!" exclaimed Claudia.

"Oh, *wait* a second!" I said suddenly. I grabbed the phone from Mary Anne. "Sam, is that you?"

"No," said the voice on the other end of the phone. "It's Jim Bartolini. I was wondering if — "

"Sam, you're a rat!" I cried. "This is important business. And furthermore, I'm telling!" I slammed the receiver down.

"The nerve!" said Mary Anne.

But Claudia and Stacey began giggling. "I think that was sort of funny," said Claudia.

"You would," I retorted.

"Oh, come on. You have to admit that was a pretty good goof call. It's better than just 'Is your refrigerator running?' or something."

"I guess," I said.

So the first Baby-sitters Club office hour (or office half hour) ended on a sour note. And the evening didn't improve much. I went home and did tell Mom what Sam had done, and Sam called me a rat, and I said, "I know you are, but what am I?" and Sam said, "I know you are, but what am I?" and I shouted, "You're driving me crazy!" and Sam shouted, "You're driving me crazy!" and Mom told Sam he couldn't use the phone for an hour and sent me to my room, which suited me fine since Watson was on his way over.

*   *   *

Shortly before Mom and Watson left on another date, I was allowed to leave my room to take a phone call. It was Claudia. "I just got a job!" she said. "Mrs. Newton called. She needed a sitter for tomorrow, so I took the job."

Mrs. Newton? "That's great, Claud," I said, but I hung up the phone feeling pretty low. *I* usually sit for Jamie. Claudia should have told the other club members when a job was offered, not just taken it herself. Just because the main phone number was hers didn't mean she got first crack at every job that came along. And how come Mrs. Newton had called *that* number after six when she was probably trying to reach me? I guessed people didn't pay much attention to hours and phone numbers, which was a shame considering all the trouble we'd gone to with our fliers and the newspaper ad. I flashed the news to Mary Anne at nine o'clock, and she flashed back TOO BAD.

Well, I thought, as I went to bed that night with Louie curled at my feet, at least I've got a new client. On Wednesday I'll get to meet Pinky and Buffy McKeever. New clients are always interesting.

If only I'd had some idea just how interesting they were going to be.

CHAPTER 7

On Wednesday afternoon, I was all set for my first job through the Baby-sitters Club. I couldn't wait to meet Pinky and Buffy. I'd never sat for twins before. I wondered what it would be like. Would they play tricks on me? And what could Pinky and Buffy be nicknames for? I'd find out soon enough.

I walked over to Quentin Court right after I got home from school. I left a little early, just in case I had any trouble finding the McKeevers' house. Mrs. McKeever had said the address was 52 Quentin Court. So I found the side of the street with the even-numbered addresses on it and started walking. There was 22 Quentin Court, 28 Quentin Court, 34, 40, 46, and sure enough, there was number 52.

I stood and looked at the house for a moment. It was a perfectly nice split-level, painted white with neat black shutters. But something was wrong. What was it? After a moment it came to me.

There were no signs of children.

There were no toys in the yard or tricycles in the driveway, no sneakers on the front stoop or artwork in the windows. I hoped Pinky and Buffy weren't going to be boring children who wanted to spend the afternoon learning about butterflies or food groups or something.

My enthusiasm was beginning to wane just a little, but I took a deep breath and marched myself straight to the front door.

Ding-dong.

Silence. No running feet or shouts like I would hear when I rang the Newtons' bell.

After a few moments, the door was opened.

A plump, pleasant-looking young woman stood on the other side of the screen, smiling. Well, I thought, at least Pinky and Buffy's mother doesn't look boring.

"Hello?" she said.

"Hi, I'm Kristy Thomas. I'm here to baby-sit for Pinky and Buffy, the twins."

There was a pause, and then the woman said, "Yes. Won't you come in?"

I stepped inside into a very pretty room. But again, something seemed wrong, and it took me a moment to figure out what it was. Then

I realized. Pinky and Buffy must have been not only very boring three-year-olds, but very careful three-year-olds. The reason the room was so pretty was because it was full of glass and china — big Oriental vases, little glass statues, even plates that were displayed on delicate stands. Everything was breakable. In our house, what with David Michael and footballs and baseballs and friends coming over all the time, breakable stuff is practically against the law.

Then I saw that the area we were standing in — the foyer and the living room — was blocked off with baby gates. That explained the china, but it didn't seem to be very nice for Pinky and Buffy.

It also occurred to me that I couldn't hear any children's voices or giggling. Suddenly I began to feel suspicious. What had I gotten myself into? The McKeevers were strangers to me. Maybe I'd been lured into — No, that was silly. At breakfast that morning, when I'd told my mother where I would be after school, she'd just raised an eyebrow. She hadn't said, Don't go, Kristy. We'll never see you again!

I smiled brightly at the woman. "So," I said. "Where are Pinky and Buffy?"

"Oh, they're in the laundry room," she replied.

The laundry room? Were they being punished? I'd gotten angry with David Michael a few times, but I'd *never* stuck him in the laundry room.

"Let me introduce myself," the woman went on. "I am Miss Hargreaves, Mrs. McKeever's niece. Mrs. McKeever is away for several days, which is why we need help with Pinky and Buffy. I have an important appointment this afternoon, and we find that we need someone with Pinky and Buffy at all times."

Well, if they were only three, what was she expecting?

"They're a bit unruly," Miss Hargreaves added.

"Ohhh," I said knowingly, wondering where the signs of unruliness were in the quiet house. "Well, that's okay. I know all about 'unruly.' I've got three brothers."

"Do you?"

I nodded. "Well, let's go let them out of the laundry room. They're probably ready to play. Maybe we could all take a walk to the brook."

"That would be lovely," replied Miss Hargreaves, "but it might be difficult for you to manage."

"Oh, I've had lots of experience."

"That's fine, then."

"Are Pinky and Buffy boys or girls?" I asked.

"Well, it doesn't much matter, of course — "

It *doesn't?*

"— but Buffy's a boy and Pinky's a girl."

"Oh, that's easy to remember," I said. I was trying to sound pleasant, but already I had a very bad case of the creeps.

"Here we are!" Miss Hargreaves announced. We were standing by a door next to the kitchen. "Now get ready. These two monsters of my aunt's will practically break the door down," she said affectionately.

My eyes opened wide. "They will?"

"Stand back."

I stood back. I wished I could stand all the way back at my house.

Miss Hargreaves opened the door. Two huge, fluffy, drooling, barking Saint Bernards hurled themselves into the hall, almost knocking each other and Miss Hargreaves over.

I shrieked. "Do I have to take care of them, too?"

"Too?" repeated Miss Hargreaves. "Who else is going to help you?"

"No, I mean, do I have to watch them *plus* Pinky and Buffy?"

"Oh, my dear! Those *are* Pinky and Buffy!"

"But — but — " I sputtered. "I'm a *baby-*sitter, not a *dog*-sitter!"

Miss Hargreaves looked confused. "I don't

know what arrangements my aunt made," she said at last, "but here are the dogs, and here *you* are, and I have to leave."

"But — but — "

"Oh, it's not *so* difficult," she went on. "They need to be outside as much as possible. Our yard isn't fenced in, so you may either take them out on their leashes, or stay with them in the backyard. If you play with them, they won't run away. Now, their footballs are in the box by the back door, their leashes are hanging on the peg above, and at four-thirty they need their chow — a can apiece — and they can each have one Mailman Cookie as a treat. The emergency numbers are posted by the phone in the kitchen, just in case. Do you have any questions?"

I shook my head dazedly.

Buffy and Pinky leaped around, galumphing after Miss Hargreaves as she put on her coat and went out to meet the cab that had come to pick her up.

Shaking, I let the dogs out in the backyard, remembering to bring their footballs. I tossed a red football gingerly toward them as they ran ahead of me. I wasn't sure what they'd do with it. Louie usually runs halfheartedly after a football and then sort of forgets to fetch it.

Not those two. They dove for the ball,

crashing into each other. One of them got it away from the other, but I couldn't tell which one. They looked identical.

I got down on my knees and clapped my hands. "Okay, boy, bring it here!" I called, not caring whether the dog was Pinky or Buffy.

Whichever one it was came barreling straight toward me. I knew that game all right. Louie likes it, too. He runs for you, then turns at the last second and veers around you. You can almost see him grinning.

But not this dog. He ran right over me. I was lost in a whirl of fur and claws and playful woofs. You really haven't lived until a dog has stepped on your face.

I sat up and rubbed my cheeks and eyes. Nothing seemed to be bleeding, so I stood up shakily. I looked around.

Oh, no. The dogs were gone! I thought Miss Hargreaves had said they would stay in the yard with me. Maybe they didn't stay with people they'd practically knocked unconscious.

"Pinky!" I shouted. "Buffy!"

Nothing.

"Pink-*eee!* Buff-*eee!*"

I ran to the front of the house. No dogs.

I looked up and down the street. No dogs.

I ran to the backyard and looked again. And

there they were. Not in the McKeevers' yard, but in the yard next door. They were racing toward me — heading for a clothesline.

"Pinky, Buffy, *no!!*"

Too late. They streaked through all the clothes and came to a screeching halt about two feet from me. One was wearing a small blanket draped over his (her?) tail. The other had a slip in his mouth.

"Bad dogs!" I cried. "Sit. . . . *Sit!*"

I took the blanket and the slip from them and glanced nervously at the house next door. It seemed pretty quiet. Maybe no one was home. Thank goodness the clothesline seemed okay except for the missing blanket and slip.

I wanted to return the things, but what about Pinky and Buffy? If I went into the other yard, would they follow me? Would they run away? I didn't know what to do. I almost didn't care. But just then a car pulled in the driveway of the house. Luckily, the driveway was on the other side of the house from where I was, but I knew I'd better do something fast. Someone could come out at any moment to bring in the laundry.

"Okay, you guys," I said to the dogs. "Look, here are your footballs." I began walking slowly backward toward the clothesline. The dogs crept after me as if they were stalking the balls.

I reached the clothesline. The dogs were still following me.

"Come on," I whispered tantalizingly. I held the balls under one arm, pinned the blanket and the slip crookedly to the line, and raced back to the McKeevers' yard at top speed.

The dogs ran after me. They liked that game.

Good for them. They could follow me all the way into the house, which was just what they did, and just where I wanted them.

We stayed inside for the rest of the afternoon, since I didn't trust the dogs outdoors anymore, even on their leashes. I watched TV. The dogs chewed on their footballs. Any time they started to get rowdy, I just held open the door to the laundry room and they calmed down. By the time Miss Hargreaves returned, I had decided something important. The members of the Baby-sitters Club should keep a notebook. Each time one of us finished a job, we should write it up in the notebook and the others should read about it. That way we could learn about each other's experiences. With a little luck, we wouldn't make any mistake more than once. For instance, no more dog-sitting.

I ran home, eager to start the notebook.

My first Baby-sitters Club job was over. I had earned three dollars and fifty cents.

CHAPTER 8

Thursday, September 25th

Kristy says we have to keep a record of every babysitting job we do in this book. My first job through the Baby-sitters Club was last Saturday. I was sitting for Jamie Newton only it wasn't just for Jamie it was for Jamie and his three cousins. Four kids altogether! Mrs. Newton didn't tell me that over the phone. Any-way, the kids were Jamie plus Rosie who was three, Brenda who was five and Rob who was eight. And boy were they wild!

Claudia didn't have an easy time of it at the Newtons', that was for sure. She called me on Sunday to tell me all about it. I was almost glad I hadn't gotten the job. What happened was that Mrs. Newton's sister, Mrs. Feldman, and her husband and their three kids were visiting, and the adults had gotten invitations to a show at an art gallery or something, so Mrs. Newton needed a baby-sitter for Jamie and his cousins. But somehow she forgot to mention that to Claudia, which wasn't at all like Mrs. Newton. It must have been because she's pregnant and thinking about the baby. Ordinarily Mrs. Newton is honest and thoughtful. She always calls her baby-sitters if there are any changes in plans. Once she even called when Jamie had come down with a cold, to ask whether I still wanted to come since I would risk catching it from him.

But things must have been slipping Mrs. Newton's mind, because when Claudia showed up that Saturday, four children were waiting for her. And there were a whole bunch of problems. Jamie and Rosie apparently didn't like each other, Brenda was cranky (*very* cranky) because she was getting over the chicken pox, and Rob hated girls, which included Rosie, Brenda, Jamie's mother, his own mother, and girl baby-sitters.

When Claudia stepped into the living room, Rob was sulking on one end of the couch, muttering things like, "Stupid girls," and, "Why do we have to have a dumb *girl* baby-sit for us?" Brenda was crying and clutching Mrs. Feldman around the legs, which made it hard for both of them to get around, and Rosie and Jamie were fighting.

Rosie was trying to yank something out of Jamie's hand.

"That's mine!" Jamie yelled indignantly.

"It is not. It's mine!" Rosie made off with her prize and charged up the stairs.

Jamie ran after her. "It is not! It's mine!"

"Mine!"

"Mine!!" shouted Jamie at the top of his lungs. (Claudia said the house was practically shaking.) "Girls don't play with trucks. That's my moving van! Give it!"

"Nonononononono!"

Since the adults hadn't left yet, Claudia wasn't sure whether she was supposed to break up the fight or let one of the parents do it. Just as she was about to dash up the stairs, Mrs. Feldman managed to unwrap Brenda from around her legs and chase after Jamie and Rosie. She took each one by the hand and walked them downstairs, explaining patiently, "Jamie, sometimes girls *do* play with trucks.

Rosie and Brenda do. But Rosie, you don't have a moving van like this one. You must have gotten confused. That belongs to Jamie — "

"*See,*" said Jamie and stuck out his tongue. Rosie stuck hers out, too.

" — so we'll get your dump truck out of the goody bag," continued Mrs. Feldman. "You brought three trucks with you, remember? Now maybe you and Jamie can play together nicely."

Jamie and Rosie looked at each other suspiciously.

Brenda burst into tears again and grabbed hold of her mother. And that's just how things were by the time Jamie's parents and the Feldmans left, except that Brenda was hugging a ratty teddy bear instead of her mother's legs.

Claudia looked around the living room nervously.

Rob looked around in disgust. His eyes fell on Jamie, who turned his back on Rosie and was pushing an ambulance back and forth, making loud siren noises. "Hey, Jamie," said Rob, "let's get away from all these *girls*, okay?" He glanced defiantly at Claudia.

" 'kay," replied Jamie vaguely, busy with the ambulance.

"Where are you going?" asked Claudia.

"I'm not telling," said Rob, and grabbed Jamie by the wrist.

Claudia dashed across the living room and blocked the doorway. Rob pulled Jamie around and hauled him off in another direction, toward the entrance to the dining room. Claudia beat him to it.

"Where are you going?" she asked him again. "I'm the baby-sitter and I have to know. Just tell me where you're going."

"Who's going to make me?"

"Nobody. But I won't let you leave until you do."

Rob whirled around again. He let go of Jamie and grabbed his sister instead. Jamie sat down on the floor in surprise.

"Have we ever had a baby-sitter as mean as *her*?" Rob asked angrily.

"No!" said Rosie.

"No," sniffled Brenda, who hadn't quite finished crying.

"Are we going to let her be mean?"

"No!" shouted his sisters.

"Okay, let's do it!"

Claudia said that her stomach felt as if it were on a roller coaster. She had no idea what the Feldman kids were going to do. She found out immediately.

Rosie began running around and around the

room, yelling at the top of her lungs. She wasn't yelling words; she was just making noise. Brenda leaped onto the Newtons' couch and jumped up and down on it as if it were a trampoline. And Rob turned his fingers into guns and aimed them at Claudia. *"Pow! Pow! Pow-pow-pow!* You're a dead man! . . . I mean, a dead lady."* Jamie looked on dazedly.

At that point, Claudia almost panicked and called Stacey for help, but Jamie, sitting quietly on the floor, inspired her. She remembered that when she was little, and she or Janine misbehaved, her mother used to turn to her father and murmur, "I-g-n-o-r-e." And they would do just that. Claudia decided to try it on the Feldmans. She sat on the floor next to Jamie, reached for a copy of *The Tale of Peter Rabbit* lying abandoned by an armchair, and began to read to him. Jamie rested his head against her shoulder.

Thump, thump, thump went Brenda.

*"Aiieeee!"*shrieked Rosie, running by Claudia and stepping in her lap. Claudia didn't even look up.

"Pow!" shouted Rob. *"Pow!* . . . Hey, baby-sitter, I'm killing you! . . . Okay? . . . Baby-sitter?"

"Not now," said Claudia. "I'm busy."

She kept reading, raising her voice when

she got to the part where Mr. McGregor chased after Peter, waving a rake.

The thumping stopped. Brenda sat down a few feet away from Claudia and tried to listen without appearing *too* interested.

Rosie continued to run around the room, but she stopped yelling, and every time she ran by Claudia she slowed up long enough to look at the pictures in the book.

By the time the story was over, Jamie, Rosie, and Brenda were as quiet as mice. Claudia moved them to the couch. She found a copy of *Where the Wild Things Are*, opened it, and read about Max putting on his wolf suit and making mischief.

"As much mischief as me?" asked Rob from across the room, dropping his guns.

"Not quite," replied Claudia. Rob looked satisfied. "If you come over here," she went on, "you can find out what happened to him."

Rob didn't say anything, but he perched on the arm of the couch and listened to the story. And to two more after that.

And that was Claudia's first Baby-sitters Club job (and the story of how she tamed the Feldmans).

CHAPTER 9

Thursday, September 25

Yesterday I babysat for Kristy's little brother, David Michael. Kristy told us to write in the Baby-Sitters Club Notebook so we could keep track of any problems we had with Baby-Sitters Club jobs, but taking care of David Michael was no trouble at all. He was very good. While Kristy was chasing around after those two elephants, Punky and Miffy, or whatever their names are, I was having a fine time with David Michael.

Ha! Stacey had a fine time at my house, all right, but she had it discovering Sam. Stacey is boy-crazy and my brother is girl-crazy. They were perfect for each other. Not that Stacey neglected David Michael. But she did talk an awful lot about Sam after Wednesday. And Sam talked a lot about Stacey. Now here's the interesting part: *Sam is in high school.* He's a freshman. And Stacey is only in seventh grade. Most high school boys wouldn't be caught dead with a lowly junior high girl — unless the girl was a knockout. So I figured that Stacey's permed hair and colorful clothes (and the fact that she came from New York City) made her pretty special.

Anyway, Stacey got to my house just as David Michael was coming home from school, and about ten minutes before I dashed off to what turned out to be my dog-sitting job. I gave her a very fast introduction to our house (not knowing whether Sam or Charlie would be home soon).

"Here's-the-kitchen-the-dishwasher's-broken-David-Michael-can-have-a-snack-cookies-in-the-jar-nothing-after-four-thirty-he's-allergic-to-chocolate-oh-here's-Louie-he-won't-be-any-trouble-all-the-phone-numbers-are-on-the-bulletin-board-Mom's-is-on-the-phone-you-know-where-I'll-be-the-TV-is-in-the-play-room-we're-not-allowed-to-watch-cable-when-Mom's-not-home-David-Michael-likes-Candy-

land-it's-in-the-cabinet-by-the-stereo-see-if-
there-are-any-notes-from-his-teacher-in-his-
lunch-box-any-questions?"

Stacey shook her head.

"Okay." I knelt in front of David Michael.
"This is Stacey," I told him. "She's my friend.
She's going to baby-sit for you today."

David Michael nodded. He's used to baby-
sitters.

"I'm going to be baby-sitting somewhere
else, not far away. I'll be back around five.
Oh, Stacey, my big brothers are Charlie and
Sam. Charlie is sixteen and Sam is fourteen. I
don't know what they're doing this afternoon.
They might be around, they might not. Have
fun, you guys!" I ran out the front door.

Stacey said that she and David Michael sat
right down at the kitchen table to have a snack.
I hadn't been gone for more than five minutes
when Sam showed up. He seemed to be angry
about something. He was slamming his fist
into a baseball glove. But he stopped short
when he saw Stacey sitting in the kitchen.
According to Sam, Stacey was a foxy chick.
According to Stacey, Sam was a gorgeous
hunk. When I heard that later, I thought about
what they looked like, and tried to figure out
what they saw in each other. (I have *absolutely*

no interest in boys, of course. Still, I realized that that kind of information might be useful some day.)

I remembered that Stacey was wearing a matching top and skirt made of gray sweat shirt material with big yellow number tens all over it. Her hair was pinned back with clips shaped like rainbows. Little silver whistles were dangling from her ears. It was all very cool, but it seemed kind of young-looking. And she was drinking a glass of milk.

I thought about Sam. Now, he *is* pretty good-looking, with dark curly hair and sparkly blue eyes and a few freckles, but he was wearing jeans so ratty he'd once promised Mom he'd throw them away (but then hadn't been able to go through with it), and a T-shirt that said: I KNOW YOU ARE, BUT WHAT AM I? To top it off, he was mad.

So where did the foxy chick and the gorgeous hunk come from? Was it the perm? The freckles?

I couldn't figure it out.

Anyway, Sam stopped being mad and Stacey finished the milk she was drinking as fast as she could, and checked to be sure she didn't have any on her upper lip.

"Hi," said Stacey.

"Hel-*lo*," said Sam. He put his books and his glove on the table, leaned against the counter, and crossed his legs, running his fingers through his hair. I've seen him do that. He thinks it makes him look cool and casual.

Stacey and Sam both spoke at once.

"I'm Stacey, Kristy's friend," said Stacey, just as Sam said, "You must be Stacey."

"Oh," said Stacey, flattered. "Has Kristy mentioned me?"

"Uh, yeah. Well, she said you were going to baby-sit today. I was going to go over to this guy Ernest's house, but maybe . . . but I think he's busy or something. So I'll just stick around here."

"Well, listen," replied Stacey, "do you want me to leave? There's no reason for your mom to pay me to baby-sit if you're going to be at home."

"No, no," said Sam quickly. "The deal with my mom is that Charlie and Kristy and I only have to baby-sit David Michael one day a week each. The rest of the time we can do whatever we want, even if we're at home."

"Wow, that's really nice of your mom."

"Can I have a Twinkie?" David Michael interrupted them.

Stacey looked at her watch. "I guess so. Do

you think you'll still be able to eat your dinner tonight?"

"Yes," replied David Michael firmly.

"Okay."

David Michael got a package of Twinkies from the cupboard, opened it, took one out, and handed the other to Sam. "Here," he said. "You want it?"

"Sure." Sam took the Twinkie, broke it in half, and gave one piece to Stacey.

"Oh . . . no, thanks," she said.

"You must be the one on the diet," Sam said. "Kristy told me one of her friends was dieting. That sure takes willpower."

"I guess." Stacey stood up. "So," she said to David Michael. "How about some Candyland?"

"Yea!"

"Heck, I'll play, too," said Sam. "We can have a championship series. First one to win two games is the Candyland Champion of the Universe."

"*You're* going to play?" David Michael's eyes widened.

"Yeah, sure."

"But you nev — "

"Hey, little brother, your shoe's untied."

"It is?" David Michael looked at his feet. He

was wearing sneakers that fastened with Velcro straps. "I don't *have* laces," he said witheringly.

"Made you look!" Sam ran out of the kitchen.

"You — you — I'm telling!" cried David Michael.

"Hey, squirt!" Sam called from the playroom. "Come on! We better start playing if we're going to have time for a championship series."

So David Michael, Stacey, and Sam settled themselves on the floor and played Candyland. They were still playing when I got home from dog-sitting. Later, in the privacy of my room, Stacey said they'd had a great time except that Sam kept teasing David Michael and accusing him of cheating. Stacey didn't know whether to laugh with Sam since she wanted to impress him, or take David Michael's side since she was his baby-sitter. She said she did both. Then I told Stacey about Pinky and Buffy McKeever, and Stacey laughed until she was practically hysterical.

All things considered, Stacey definitely had the easiest of the first four Baby-sitters Club jobs. Mary Anne's, which was next, was sort of scary, as you'll see. And it was pretty interesting . . . at least to me.

CHAPTER 10

Saturday, September 27

I don't know what Kristy always makes such a fuss about. Watson's kids are cute. Karen is five and Andrew is three. I think Kristy would like them if she ever baby-sat for them. Are you reading this Kristy? I hope so. Well, Kristy said this notebook is for us to write our experiences and our problems in, especially our problems.

And there were a few

problems at Watson's house. When I said Andrew and Karen were cute, I meant they were cute-looking. They were cute-acting, too, most of the time. But sometimes Karen was a pill. That was one problem. Another problem was Boo-Boo, the cat. The biggest problem was Mrs. Porter, the next-door neighbor. Anyone else who sits for Andrew and Karen should know about Boo-Boo and Mrs. Porter ahead of time.

Watson picked Mary Anne up at 8:45 Saturday morning and drove her to his house. He lives all the way across Stoneybrook, so it's hard to get to his place by bike.

According to Mary Anne, Watson was very nice to her in the car, which was to be expected. He always makes an extra effort to be nice to me, since he knows I don't like to have him around, so of course he would be nice to my best friend.

Mary Anne says that Watson lives in a very pretty, big house. I guess he has a lot of money. He'd have to, the way he throws it around, buying Chinese food right and left, and taking my mom out on dates almost every night. Anyway, the house is large, and Andrew and Karen have neat rooms. And *toys*. Mary Anne had never seen so many — gigantic stuffed animals, dolls, a train that you could really ride around the backyard, cars, bikes, a playhouse, costumes to dress up in. It was incredible, kind of like being in Toys 'R' Us.

Watson turned out to be not only a very good father, but a very organized customer. The first thing he did was introduce Mary Anne to Andrew and Karen, whose mother had just brought them over. Then he showed her their rooms, took her back downstairs, showed her where all the stuff was for making lunch, and finally pinned up a list of phone numbers she might need.

And then he brought out Boo-Boo.

From what Mary Anne told me, Boo-Boo must truly be a boo-boo. What a mess of a cat. He was gray with big yellow eyes that were kind of handsome, but he was *fat*. He looked like a pillow with legs attached. When he stood up, his stomach touched the ground, and when he tried to run, it swayed back and forth. He was gross.

"He weighs seventeen pounds," Karen said proudly.

"We think he belongs in the *Guinness Book of World Records*," remarked Watson.

Mary Anne couldn't figure out why Watson was showing Boo-Boo to her. Okay, he was really, really fat. So what? Certainly he didn't need to be fed.

Watson cleared his throat and adjusted his glasses. "There are a few things you should know about Boo-Boo," he said.

Now, Mary Anne is not the bravest person in the world, and she said that right then she began to feel just the teensiest bit afraid. She put her finger in her mouth and bit at the nail.

"The first thing," said Watson, "is that Boo-Boo bites if provoked. And scratches."

"He's an attack cat," added Karen.

"It's best if you just steer clear of him," Watson went on. "I'd offer to confine him while I'm gone, but he doesn't like that much."

"He gnawed the laundry room door all up," said Karen.

"Just try to ignore him."

Mary Anne nodded.

"Whatever you do, don't touch him," added Watson.

Mary Anne nodded again.

"Well, I guess that's it. Any questions?"

"No, not really. Lunch at twelve-thirty, right?" said Mary Anne.

"Right."

"What about Mrs. Porter, Daddy?" asked Karen.

"Oh, I think she's on vacation," replied Watson. "No need to worry about her." He turned to Mary Anne. "Mrs. Porter is an elderly woman who lives next door. She's a bit on the eccentric side and Karen is convinced she's a witch. She isn't, of course, but she doesn't like animals and Boo-Boo seems to have gotten on her bad side. We try to keep the two of them apart. Okay, I'm off, kids." Watson kissed Andrew and Karen good-bye. "I'll be home by one-thirty," he told Mary Anne.

Mary Anne was just wondering how to entertain her charges when Karen began to talk. It turned out that she was a nonstop chatterer. "We're divorced," she announced.

"Yup," said Andrew.

"Our parents live in different houses."

"Yup," said Andrew. He sat down in a little wagon.

"Our mommy's going to get married again."

"Yup," said Andrew, pushing himself around the playroom.

"Then we'll have one mommy and two daddies."

"Yup," said Andrew. He backed into a bookcase.

"And if our daddy gets married again, then how many mommies and daddies will we have, Andrew?"

"Yup."

Mary Anne giggled. "Come on, you guys. It's a sunny day. Let's play outside, okay?"

"Oh, great!" exclaimed Karen. "I have a new doll. Daddy bought her for me. She hasn't been out in the sun much yet. I think she should get a tan, don't you? Dolls can tan, you know. Of course, they're real anyway. They can do whatever people do. They can draw and breakdance and. . . ."

Mary Anne was beginning to feel dizzy. "Want to play outside, Andrew?"

"Yup."

Mary Anne took the kids into Watson's big backyard. Andrew brought the wagon and pushed Boo-Boo around in it.

"Is he allowed to do that?" Mary Anne asked Karen. "Your father said not to touch Boo-Boo."

"Oh, he meant *you* shouldn't touch Boo-Boo. You're a stranger. But Boo-Boo knows us. He wouldn't hurt us." Karen paused for a breath and went on. "You see that house? The one next door?"

Mary Anne peered over Watson's rose gardens and between the trees. Next door was a sprawling Victorian mansion, with gables and turrets and wooden curlicues on the porch. The paint was peeling and one shutter was crooked. Mary Anne said later that it looked dark and scary.

"Yes?" she said to Karen.

"That's where the witch lives, right, Andrew?"

Andrew plowed the wagon into a tree and Boo-Boo leaped out. "Yup."

"It's Mrs. Porter, and she's an honest-and-truly witch. Mrs. Porter isn't her witch name, though. Her witch name is Morbidda Destiny. The big kids on the street told me so. And she eats toads and casts spells and flies to witch meetings on her broomstick every midnight."

Mary Anne stared at the house, nibbling away at her nails again. She wasn't sure what to tell Karen. If she told her the stories weren't true, she probably wouldn't get off to a very good start as a baby-sitter. If she agreed with

Karen, she'd practically be lying to her. At last she asked, "Do you believe in the stories about Morb — Mrs. Porter?"

Karen nodded. "I have proof."

"You do?"

"Yup. The proof is Boo-Boo. Mrs. Porter made him fat. One day when Boo-Boo was nice and skinny, he went into Mrs. Porter's garden and dug up some of her flowers. Mrs. Porter came out and yelled at him and threw a fit. The next day he started getting fat."

"Yup," said Andrew.

"So now we have to keep Boo-Boo away from Mrs. Porter's house. We don't want her to cast another spell on him. Making him fat wasn't so bad, but she might do something really, really mean."

"Well," said Mary Anne, "we don't have to worry about it today since Mrs. Porter's not at home."

And it was at that *exact* second that Mary Anne saw a window shade snap up on the first floor of Mrs. Porter's house. A wrinkled face with a big nose pressed itself against the panes of glass.

Karen saw the face, too. "Augh!" she screamed. "That's Morbidda Destiny! She's home after all! Where's Boo-Boo? Where's Boo-Boo?"

Mary Anne began to feel afraid again. She knew there were no such things as witches (were there?), but the face at the window didn't look very friendly. And Andrew was crying, and Karen was panicking.

"All right." Mary Anne tried to remain calm. She thought about what Watson had told her — that Mrs. Porter was just an eccentric old lady. "Let's look for Boo-Boo, you guys," she said.

"We don't have to," wailed Karen. "I see him. He's — " Karen gulped. She pointed her finger. "He's in Morbidda Destiny's garden!"

"Well, I'll just go get him — somehow," said Mary Anne, remembering that she wasn't supposed to touch Boo-Boo, let alone pick him up.

"She's already gone from the window!" Karen cried. "She's coming to the door! I know it."

"Okay, okay. Karen, you're in charge of Andrew for a few minutes. You stay in the yard with him and watch him. I'll be right back."

Mary Anne said her heart was pounding as she crossed Watson's yard and stood at the edge of Mrs. Porter's property. Boo-Boo was about ten feet away from her in the middle of some chrysanthemums, digging away happily.

"Boo-Boo," Mary Anne called softly. She glanced at the house. No sign of Mrs. Porter. Maybe she hadn't seen Boo-Boo. "Boo-Boo," Mary Anne called again. "Come here." She snapped her fingers.

Boo-Boo didn't even look up.

"Yoo-hoo! Boo-Boo!" Mary Anne stepped closer. Boo-Boo sat down and scratched himself. "Boo-Boo. Hey, fat cat!"

"Boo-Boo. Hey, fat cat!" called a croaky voice.

Mary Anne's heart just about stopped beating. She whirled around. As she was whirling, she could hear Karen shrieking in Watson's yard. Behind Mary Anne stood . . . a witch. "Honest to goodness," she told me later. "She looked just like a witch from a picture book."

Mrs. Porter, or Morbidda Destiny or whoever she was, was dressed in black from head to toe. Her hair was gray and frazzly. There was a wart on the end of her nose. She was carrying what Mary Anne at first mistook for a broom, but which turned out to be a rake.

"That fat cat," said Mrs. Porter, shaking the rake with every word, "is digging up my mums."

"I know, I know. I'm sorry. I'm trying to get him out for you." Mary Anne decided to forget Watson's warning. She stepped right into the garden and reached for Boo-Boo.

Boo-Boo hissed and swiped at her with his paw, claws extended.

Mary Anne jumped back.

"That does it, girlie," said Mrs. Porter. She jumped into the garden and waved the rake at Boo-Boo.

Boo-Boo's eyes opened wide. He leaped over a bush of golden mums, and streaked away. Luckily, he streaked back into Watson's yard.

Mrs. Porter shook her rake after him. "Rapscallion!" she cried. She headed for her house. Mary Anne could hear her muttering things like, "Children and pets," and, "Darned nuisance."

Back in Watson's yard, Karen greeted Mary Anne tearfully. "Did you hear that? It was a curse!"

"What was? 'Rapscallion'?" Mary Anne asked, looking nervously over her shoulder at the chrysanthemum bed.

"Yeah!"

"No, that wasn't a curse. That's a real word. She was calling Boo-Boo a name, but she did *not* put a spell on him."

"Are you sure?"

"Positive. Right, Andrew?"

"Yup."

"I don't know," said Karen. "I don't know."

"Look," Mary Anne went on. "Did you see Morb — Mrs. Porter mixing up herbs or looking for bats' feet?"

"No. . . ."

"Did you see her crushing toadstools or stirring things in a caldron?"

"No. . . ."

"Then how do you know she cast a spell?" asked Mary Anne triumphantly.

"She's a witch. She can do anything she w — Hey!" shrieked Karen, pointing.

Mary Anne's stomach flip-flopped. She immediately looked over at Mrs. Porter's yard, sure she was going to see the old woman flapping across the lawn in her funny black dress. But Mrs. Porter wasn't in sight. Karen was pointing at Boo-Boo.

"Look at that!" cried Karen. "He's going crazy."

Boo-Boo did, in fact, look a little crazy, Mary Anne said later. As she watched, the cat ran partway across Watson's backyard, came to an abrupt stop, ran around in a circle, then dashed off in the direction he had just come from and scrambled up a tree.

"Oh," said Mary Anne nervously, "he's just being a cat. Cats do silly things like that all the time." Mary Anne had never owned a cat, so she'd had very little experience with them, but she had once seen the Pikes' cat, Sarge, wake up from a sound sleep, leap off the couch, jump up on top of the television set, and immediately fall asleep again. Still. . . .

"*Boo-Boo* doesn't do silly things," said Karen, edging toward Mary Anne. "He's too fat and old."

Mary Anne took Karen and Andrew by their hands. The three of them stood and watched Boo-Boo. For a while he looked as if he might go to sleep up in the tree.

Karen grew bored. "Psst," she whispered after a moment. "Morbidda Destiny's at her window again — and she's looking over here."

Sure enough, the old face was pressed against the windowpanes. Morbidda raised her right hand to her nose . . .

. . . and Boo-Boo sat straight up, slipped, slid, and finally fell out of the tree, landed on his feet, and shot past Mary Anne and the kids, hissing as he went by.

"Oh, *nooooo*," wailed Karen. Mary Anne squeezed her hand.

Boo-Boo tore up the steps to the back porch and waited by the door.

"I guess it would be a good idea to let him in," said Mary Anne. "At least we won't have to worry about Mrs. Porter's garden anymore."

So Mary Anne opened the door and Boo-

Boo ran inside. He ran straight into the laundry room, jumped into the laundry basket, and stayed there while Mary Anne and Karen and Andrew ate lunch. Every time Mary Anne checked on him, he peered at her through the sides of the basket and yowled.

Mary Anne started to tell Karen that it was all just a big coincidence, but then she didn't know how to explain the meaning of coincidence, so she gave up.

"Daddy, it's a spell," Karen told Watson urgently as soon as he came home.

Watson laughed. "Don't be silly. There are no such things as spells."

But by then, even Mary Anne wasn't so sure. She was very relieved to go home.

CHAPTER 11

On the Wednesday after Mary Anne baby-sat for Watson's kids, Claudia, Mary Anne, Stacey, and I were holding a regular meeting of the Baby-sitters Club in Claudia's room. It was 5:45 and the phone had rung twice. The first call had been Mrs. McKeever who was back in Stoneybrook. I'd said that, although Pinky and Buffy were very nice, we were not pet-sitters. The second call had been a new customer. Stacey had answered the phone. "Hello. Baby-sitters Club."

"Hello, my name is Mrs. Marshall," said the voice on the other end. "I live over on Rosedale. I got your flier, and I need a baby-sitter for Friday night. I'm sorry it's such short notice, but we had a baby-sitter lined up, and he had to cancel."

"Oh, that's okay," said Stacey. "Maybe I

should tell you some things about the club, though, first. There are four of us and we're all twelve years old. On Friday nights, we can sit until ten. Well, one of us can."

"Oh, that's fine," replied Mrs. Marshall. "My husband and I are just going out for dinner. We should be home around nine-thirty."

"Okay," said Stacey. "And how many children do you have?"

"Two."

"And how old are they?"

"Nina is three and Eleanor is one."

"Do you have any pets?"

(Some people seem a little surprised when we ask this question, but Mrs. Marshall was okay about it.) "We have a cat. He's no trouble at all."

"And is there anything special the baby-sitter should know, or that she'd have to do?"

Mrs. Marshall paused. (Aha! There's always a catch.) "Well, you'll have to give Eleanor her eardrops. She's getting over an ear infection. She always cries and puts up a fuss, but in the end, she holds still and lets us put the drops in."

That didn't sound too bad. "Okay," said Stacey. "Let me find out who's available and I'll call you right back."

102

As you can see, we'd learned a lot over the last couple of weeks.

Claudia took the job, since Stacey was mysteriously busy that night (she wouldn't tell us exactly what she was doing), and Mary Anne's father and my mother get hysterical if we're not home by 9:30 on the dot. If Claudia was a little late, the Kishis wouldn't mind (much).

After we called Mrs. Marshall back, I said, "Hey, why don't we figure out how much money we've earned on our Baby-sitters Club jobs?"

"Okay!" said Stacey. She loved anything to do with money. Claudia handed her a piece of paper and a pencil. Then I opened our record book and read out the amount of money we'd been paid for each job. The total came to $26.75.

"Hey, that's not bad!" I exclaimed. "You know what we should do? We should each donate about three dollars and we could have a pizza party on Saturday afternoon."

"Yeah, a celebration of our club," said Claudia excitedly, "because it's a success!"

"We'll get Coke and M&Ms," I said.

"All the junk food we can eat," added Mary Anne happily.

Stacey remained silent.

"Oh, Stace," I said suddenly. "I'm sorry.

We forgot about your diet. Maybe — "

"Oh, never mind." Stacey cut me off. "I may not be able to go anyway. We're, um, going to — to New York on Friday and we might not be back in time for the party."

"Didn't you just go to New York?" asked Claudia.

"Well, yes, but there are a lot of things to finish up. The move and all."

Claudia frowned. "I thought you said you finally got everything straightened out."

"Oh. We — we have to see some friends, too. Oh, wow, it's six. I better go. Bye, you guys!"

Stacey tore out of Claudia's house.

Claudia and Mary Anne and I just looked at one another.

When I got home that evening, I found Watson parked on our living room couch reading the paper like he lived at our house or something. I couldn't help making a face. Luckily, Watson didn't see it. In fact, he didn't look up from the paper until I was tiptoeing past the living room, trying to sneak into the kitchen without having to speak to him.

"Well, hi there, Kristy," he said cheerfully.

"Hi," I replied. I paused for a second, trying

to decide whether I should say anything else, then gave up, and went on into the kitchen.

Mom must have just gotten home. She was reaching into the refrigerator, pulling out vegetables and leftovers for dinner. "Hi, sweetheart," she said. "How was school?"

"It was fine. Um, Mom, Watson's in our living room."

Mom smiled at me. "I know, silly. He came home with me. I picked him up after work."

"Is he staying for dinner?"

Mom began slicing a tomato. "Yes, he is."

"Do you know this is the third time he's been over for dinner in the last week?"

"Kristy. . . ."

"What did he bring us this time? Greek food? Italian?"

"Nothing," replied Mom smoothly. "He's here for leftovers."

That was definitely not a good sign. It meant Watson was through trying to impress us, and that Mom didn't feel she had to impress Watson anymore, either. It meant they were getting more comfortable with each other. And it meant that Watson probably felt pretty comfortable with my brothers and me. Not a good sign at all.

Mom eyed me.

"What?" I said.

"Honey, would you please run upstairs and put on a dress?"

"A *dress!* Why?" I thought I looked all right in my school clothes. Besides, I never wear dresses if I can help it.

"Because I'm the mommy, that's why."

I giggled. Mom has a red T-shirt with that slogan across the front.

"Put on the blue and white one we just bought, okay?"

I sighed. "Okay."

When I got upstairs, all my brothers were there brushing their hair. They had changed into decent shirts and pants. "What's going on?" I asked Sam.

He shrugged. "Something to do with Watson. Mom told us to dress up."

I made another face. I'm pretty good at faces. One thing I can do that no one else in our entire grade can do — not even the boys — is turn my eyelids inside out. I did that then.

"Kristy, grow up," said Charlie. "That is really gross."

"It's scary," added David Michael.

"Sorry," I said. I helped him button his shirt.

Then I changed into my blue and white dress, purposely didn't brush my hair, and went downstairs. My brothers were helping

Mom and Watson set the table in the dining room. Mom was lighting candles.

"Mom," I said, "will you please tell me what's happening? Why is everything so fancy?"

"Because we're celebrating."

"We're celebrating with leftover Spaghetti-O's?"

"It doesn't matter what we eat. I just want us feeling festive."

"Why? What are we getting festive about?"

Mom and Watson glanced at each other. Watson winked. "You'll see," said Mom.

"Mom, I don't feel too well," I said suddenly.

My mother sized me up in one half of a second. "Save it, Kristy," she said.

"Okay, okay, okay."

A few minutes later, we were sitting around the dining room table, which looked almost as fancy as it does at Thanksgiving. Mom had spread out a green tablecloth and put a white runner over it. We were eating off of our good china, and everyone had a wine goblet. Mom and Watson were the only ones with wine in their wine goblets, though. David Michael's and mine were filled with milk. Sam and Charlie had put Gatorade in theirs.

Spaghetti-O's and Gatorade. Some dinner.

We began passing around the leftovers. Mom and Watson didn't pay a bit of attention to what we kids chose for dinner. When everyone was served, Mom stood up at the head of the table and raised her glass. "Something very special happened today," she said.

I drew in my breath.

"Watson asked me if I would consider getting engaged to him."

I let the breath out.

"That's great, Mom," said Sam.

"Congratulations," said Charlie.

"Yea!" cried David Michael, getting into the spirit of things.

"What does that mean?" I asked.

"It means your mother won't even let me give her an engagement ring yet," said Watson, smiling.

Smart move, Mom, I thought.

"But that I'm thinking about it," added Mom.

"Well," said Sam, "if engagement is one step away from marriage, does this mean you're two steps away?"

Mom and Watson laughed. "I guess so," said Mom.

Good. Keep it that way.

"If you got married," I asked, "where would we live?"

"I don't know, honey," replied Mom. "We haven't thought that far ahead."

"Would we have to change schools?"

"I don't — "

"Would Karen and Andrew live with us, too? Would you keep on working? Would Dad still give you child-support money?"

"Kristy, I *don't know*. Now, enough questions. This is a celebration. We'll worry about those things later. Eat your — what is that you're eating?"

"Twinkies," I replied. "Twinkies and fried chicken."

"Eat your Twinkies and fried chicken."

At that, everybody laughed.

I managed a tiny, forced smile. Very forced. I couldn't believe Mom's news. Why would she want to risk getting married again? My only hope was that she'd see the light before it was too late, and let our family return to normal.

CHAPTER 12

The Baby-sitters Club planned its pizza party for Saturday afternoon. On Friday, during a regular meeting of the club, we pooled our money, except we only had nine dollars instead of twelve. That was because Stacey wasn't at the meeting. She and her parents had pulled out of their driveway right after Stacey and I came home from school. Stacey waved to Claudia and me from the car window as they drove by us.

"They're on their way to New York," Claudia said. "Stacey told me at lunch today that they might be back tomorrow morning, or they might not be back until the evening."

"I wonder what we should do about the party."

"I don't know," replied Claudia slowly.

"Let's talk about it at the meeting."

So we did.

"I think we should wait," said Mary Anne, curling up on Claudia's bed and pulling a pack of Juicy Fruit out of the pillowcase. "It'll be more fun if the whole club's at the party. We can have the party next weekend."

"But we really want to have it tomorrow, right?" said Claudia.

"Right," Mary Anne and I replied.

"So why don't we go ahead and buy everything except the pizzas tomorrow morning. If Stacey comes home, we can order the pizzas at the last minute and have the party. If she doesn't, we'll keep the stuff until next weekend. Okay?"

So that was what we agreed to do. And that was what we *tried* to do. But it never happened.

The next morning, everything went wrong. Our house was in chaos. David Michael woke up with a stomach virus. Louie went streaking through the downstairs, skidded on a throw rug, and hurt his paw. Mom was grouchy, Charlie couldn't find his football helmet, and Sam overslept and nearly missed an emergency meeting of the Math Club.

I myself was doing fine until the phone started ringing. The first call was from Mary

Anne. She was crying. "Mmfawolemspoo-munno," she wailed.

"What? Mary Anne, I can't understand you. What's wrong?"

She slowed down and tried again.

"Your father?" I repeated. "Won't let you . . . spend your money . . . on what? On the *feet* of a *pauper*? . . . Oh, on the pizza party. . . . Oh, Mary *Anne*. You're kidding. Can't you talk to him?"

"I *tried*."

"Why won't he let you?"

"He says I should save the money I earn for more important, necessary things, like clothes and college."

"You mean you have to start paying for your clothes *yourself*?"

"I don't know. I don't think he does, either. He just won't let me spend three dollars on pizza. That's all."

"What a meanie."

"Yeah." Mary Anne blew her nose.

"Well, Claudia's got all the money. She can give yours back. We'll still have nine dollars when we get Stacey's share. I guess the four of us can make do with one large pizza. Stacey probably won't eat any, anyway."

"But Kristy, I'm not coming to the party now," said Mary Anne.

"Why not?"

"I'm not letting you guys pay for ev — Just a second," she whispered. Then, "Okay, thanks for helping me with this math," Mary Anne said loudly. "Now I understand what we're doing."

"Did your father just walk in?" I asked.

"Yes."

"Do you have to get off the phone now?"

"Yes. Listen, thanks again. I'll see you in school on Monday. Bye, June."

"June? Bye, Mary Anne."

So Mary Anne was the first person to drop out of the party.

The second phone call was from Claudia, who wasn't crying, but sounded like she might have been, or might be going to. "Guess what," she said angrily.

"What?"

"Mom and Dad got a letter from school in the mail this morning saying how I'm not trying hard enough and don't pay attention and if I'd just concentrate on my work I could be a very good student."

"So? Don't you get one of those letters every fall?"

"Yeah, but this time Dad had read it right before I told him and Mom about the pizza party, and he said no parties for me, it was time I started being more serious, and did I have any homework this weekend? When I said yes, he said he wanted me to spend all weekend on it."

"*All* weekend on ten math problems?"

"Well, and on catching up on all the homework I didn't do so far this year."

"Oh."

"I'm sorry, Kristy."

"Me, too. But Mary Anne can't come either. I guess the party's off."

"Maybe not. I'm not through with my parents yet. Let's not say the party's off unless Stacey doesn't come home in time."

"Fine with me."

"All right. I'm going to go start some of the math. Now here's a question for you. When do you think we will ever need to know how to multiply fractions?"

"I don't know."

"Have you ever seen anyone besides teachers and math students do it?"

"No."

"Do you need to do it in order to go shopping, cook dinner, or baby-sit?"

"No."

"I rest my case. School is stupid."

"Good-bye, Claudia."

"Good-bye."

The weirdest thing that morning happened with Stacey. Around 11:30, I decided to call the McGills to find out if they were home yet. Mrs. McGill answered the phone and I introduced myself to her and asked for Stacey. There was a pause, then it sounded as if Mrs. McGill might be covering up the mouthpiece of the phone, and then she got back on the line and said, "I'm sorry, dear, Stacey's not home."

"Oh," I said, disappointed. "Where did she go?"

"Well, she's . . . um . . . she stayed in New York with friends, Kristy. She'll be back tomorrow night."

"Oh. Thank you," I said glumly. As soon as I hung up, the phone rang again. "Hello?" I said.

"Hi, it's me." Mary Anne.

"Hi! Did your father change his mind?"

"Are you kidding? I just wanted to be sure you knew Stacey was home. I was riding my bike to the Pikes' — that's where I am now; they called and asked me to sit this morning — and the McGills passed me in their car. Stacey didn't see me, though."

"Mary Anne, are you *sure* you saw Stacey in the car?" I said.

"Yeah, positive. She was sitting in the back

115

wearing Claudia's fedora. Why?"

"Because I just spoke to Mrs. McGill. She said Stacey decided to stay in New York with friends. Something funny is going on."

"Yeah," said Mary Anne slowly. *"Some-body's lying. And it isn't me."*

"Yeah . . . and it may not be *only* Mrs. McGill," I added.

"What do you mean?" asked Mary Anne. "And make it quick. I've got to get off in a second."

"I mean that Stacey must have told her mother what to say. Mothers don't usually lie on their own. Stacey's so weird about food and dieting. She didn't want to come to the party in the first place. What is it with her, anyway?"

"I don't know, but I gotta go. Bye!"

I punched the button on the phone and quickly began dialing again — just as Mom came into the kitchen, still looking grouchy.

"Kristy," she said, "how long have you been on that phone this morning?"

"On *this* phone? For about an hour. On the hot line to the White House, for about — "

"Kristy . . . " said Mom warningly.

"Sorry. How's David Michael?" I asked.

"Better already. I think his bug will be short-lived."

116

"That's good." I turned back to the phone. "Kristy. . . ."

"Just one more call, Mom. It's important."

"Okay, *one* call. You know, you can go *over* to Mary Anne's and Claudia's. It's not as if they lived in Europe."

"Okay, okay. Last one." I dialed Claudia's number and she answered on the first ring.

"I'm trying to do my homework," she informed me crossly.

"This'll be short, I promise," I said. "There's something weird with Stacey. Mary Anne saw the McGills come home a little while ago, with Stacey in the backseat. But when I called them, Mrs. McGill told me Stacey had decided to stay in New York. I think Stacey was right there by the phone and just doesn't want to go to the party."

"Hmm," said Claudia, sounding puzzled. "I don't know what that means. But if Mary Anne can't come to the party, and Stacey doesn't want to, and I'm not allowed to, I guess there's not much point in trying to have it."

"No," I agreed. We both got off the phone feeling depressed.

Immediately, the phone rang again.

"*Kristy!*" shouted my mother. "Enough with the phone!"

"Do you want to answer it, Mom?" I asked. "I'm tired of it."

"All right." Mom lifted the receiver. "Hello?" she said brusquely, and then softly, "Oh, hello."

It had to be Watson.

"How are you? . . . Yes? . . . Oh, no. . . . Well, David Michael is sick. . . . The Baby-sitters Club? Let me check with Kristy. . . . What? . . . I don't know. I guess so. Sure. . . . Twenty minutes. Someone will be ready. Good-bye, sweetheart.

"Kristy," Mom said before she'd even hung up the phone. "There's a little emergency. Watson needs one of you girls immediately. He needs someone to sit for his kids this afternoon. I'd tell him to drop them off here instead, but I'm afraid they'd catch David Michael's virus." "

"Oh, Mom!" I cried. "It'll have to be *me*."

I didn't have a choice.

CHAPTER 13

Exactly twenty minutes later, Watson drove up with two little kids in the backseat. Mom ran me out to the car and practically shoved me in next to Watson. The emergency was that Watson's ex-wife (Andrew and Karen's mother) had fallen and broken her ankle and was in the emergency room at the hospital. Watson had to go over there and do something about insurance forms (I think) and also wait with her and take her home and make sure she could use the crutches okay and everything, since her future second husband was away for the weekend. Watson didn't want to make the kids hang around the hospital with him.

Watson put his foot on the accelerator and vroomed us down the driveway. I've never seen anyone in such a big hurry — and all over a broken ankle. If Watson could have flown the car back to his house I think he would have.

I wondered how Mom felt, seeing Watson go rushing off to his ex-wife. But I knew Watson's divorce was a friendly one, and also that some things (like insurance) still had to be straightened out. But Mom must have felt a little funny, anyway.

Watson talked a mile a minute during the drive, trying to tell me everything I'd need to know. I was glad I'd read the Baby-sitters Club Notebook, though, because he didn't say anything about Mrs. Porter, the witch next door, or Boo-Boo the attack cat. I planned to keep the kids inside — or at least to keep Boo-Boo inside.

"The children are Andrew and Karen," said Watson breathlessly. "Andrew is three and Karen is five. They're about ready for their lunch. Peanut butter and jelly is fine. Karen can help you find things. Emergency numbers are by the phone, but since I'll be at the hospital, if there's a real emergency it would probably be easier to call your mom."

"Okay," I said, feeling a bit dazed.

"Around two o'clock, Andrew goes down for a nap. I guess that's all you need to know. I wish I could take the time to show you everything, but Karen will have to fill in for me, okay, pumpkin?"

"Okay!" said Karen.

"Good girl." Watson screeched to a halt in front of a big white house in one of the fanciest neighborhoods in Stoneybrook. A wide green lawn stretched all around it, interrupted by old trees and little flower gardens. I looked for the witch's house as I got out of the car. "Be good kids," said Watson. "And Kristy, thank you. I want you to know that I really appreciate this."

I held the back door open and Andrew and Karen scrambled out of the car. "See you later!" called Watson. He peeled off.

I stood in Watson's front yard and looked at Andrew and Karen. Baby-sitting for them was absolutely the last thing I wanted to do.

I sighed heavily. "All right. Are you guys hungry?"

"Starving," said Karen. "You know what I had for breakfast? Just toast. Toast and orange juice. I wanted Pop-Tarts, but Mommy said no 'cause they're junk food. Sometimes Daddy lets us have them, though. He does and Mommy doesn't. Isn't that silly? I think it's really silly."

"Are *you* hungry, Andrew?" I asked.

"Yup."

"Well, let's go get some lunch, then."

We went through the front door of Watson's house, and the first thing I saw was not the huge, gorgeous front hall, not the tree that was growing in the living room, not the sparkling chandelier or the stained glass window, but a fat creature that could only be Boo-Boo.

Sure enough. "Hi, Boopa-de-Boo," cried Karen, hugging him. "This is Boo-Boo," she told me. "He's Daddy's cat. He's real old. Daddy had him even before he knew our mommy. Did you know he's had two spells put on him by a *witch*? She lives next door in the scary house."

I sighed again. It was going to be a long day. "Come on. Let's get our lunch," I said.

In the kitchen, Karen helped me find the stuff for sandwiches, and then I fixed apple slices and carrot sticks and poured us each a glass of milk.

"Yum," said Karen. "Yummy-yummers! You're a neat baby-sitter. You fix good food."

"Yup," said Andrew.

Karen ate a few bites of her sandwich, then suddenly looked at me very seriously, her brown eyes glistening. "Is our mommy all right?" she asked me.

"Oh, of *course*," I replied. "A broken ankle isn't too serious. She'll have to wear a cast and walk on crutches for a while, but in a few weeks she'll be all better. Having a cast is fun. Everyone signs it and draws pictures on it."

"Did you ever have a cast?" asked Karen.

"Last summer," I replied. "I broke my ankle, just like your mommy."

"How did you do it?"

"I was taking our dog, Louie, for a walk —"

"You have a dog? Can I see him sometime?" interrupted Karen, wiping away a milk-mustache.

"I guess," I answered. "Anyway, I was taking Louie for a walk, except I was riding my bike. Louie was on his leash running next to me. We came to a tree, Louie went one way, I went the other, the leash wrapped around the tree, and *whoosh!* I flew off my bike."

Karen giggled. Even solemn Andrew managed a tiny smile. I was beginning to feel better. Mary Anne was right. Karen and Andrew weren't too bad — considering Watson was their father.

"So that's how I broke my ankle. I had to wear a cast for six weeks. I couldn't go swimming all summer."

"Yuck," said Karen.

"Yuck," said Andrew. It was a nice change from, "Yup." He went back to his lunch, which he was eating slowly and neatly. Take a bite, chew, chew, chew, chew, chew, chew, chew, swallow, wipe mouth, start over.

Karen ate silently, too, for a moment, and I could tell she was thinking about something. At last she put the remains of her sandwich on her plate and said, "You're Kristy, right?"

"Right," I replied.

"Is your mommy Edie Thomas?"

"That's right." The kid was smart.

"My daddy says he loves your mommy."

"I guess," I said uncomfortably. I realized that Karen looked uncomfortable, too.

"If they get married, your mommy will be my mommy."

"Stepmommy, I mean stepmother," I corrected her. "And guess what. I'd be your stepsister. And yours, Andrew."

"Yup," said Andrew.

Karen thought for a while again. "That would be okay," she said at last. And then, "Do you like being divorced, Kristy?"

"Not particularly," I said.

"How come?"

"Because I never see my father. He moved to California. That's far away."

"Ooh," said Karen. "We don't like being divorced either, but we get to see our daddy lots."

"I know," I said dryly. Boy, did I know.

Watson, the perfect divorced father.

"Our mommy's getting married again."

"I know."

"We don't want her to, do we, Andrew?"

"Yup."

"You don't?" I said.

"Nope. Mommy says oh we're so lucky, we'll have two daddies, and maybe someday two daddies and two mommies. But we just want our old mommy and daddy — all in one house."

"I know what you mean." Karen was all right.

Suddenly I was aware of little sniffling sounds next to me. Andrew was crying into his sandwich crusts. Karen jumped up and ran around the table to hug her brother. "I'm sorry, Andrew," she said. "I'm sorry."

"What's wrong?" I asked nervously.

"He doesn't like to hear about all the mommies and daddies. I'm not 'asposed to talk about it too much."

"Oh." I wiped Andrew's tears with my napkin. "Hey, you guys, how about a special treat? Ice cream for dessert!"

"At *lunchtime?*" asked Karen incredulously.

"Sure," I said, opening the freezer door and hoping I'd find ice cream inside. Luckily, there was almost a whole quart of cookies 'n' cream.

"Divorced kids are special kids. How about it, Andrew?"

Andrew's eyes lit up. "Okay," he sniffled. "That's good."

"All *right!*" I ruffled his hair.

I placed three bowls of cookies 'n' cream ice cream on the table and we ate away happily. Karen was so happy, she couldn't even speak. As we were slurping up the last dribbles, Boo-Boo waddled into the kitchen. Karen jumped up and ran to the back door.

"Wait!" I cried. "Karen, don't let him out, okay?"

"But he wants to go. He's allowed."

"Is Mrs. Porter home?" I asked.

Karen stepped away from the door. "Oh. . . . I don't know."

"Maybe we better keep him inside. Just until your dad comes back, okay?"

"Yeah," said Karen. "Good idea."

"But *we* can go out," I added. I decided that would be all right, as long as we didn't go near Mrs. Porter's yard.

"Because divorced kids are special kids," said Andrew.

"You got it," I said.

Andrew giggled. "You got it? That's funny!"

Andrew and Karen and I played hide-and-seek until it was time for Andrew's nap. Then

Karen and I sat on the back porch and read *Little Toot* and *The Snowy Day* and *The Tale of Mrs. Tiggy-Winkle.* We were halfway through *The Little Engine That Could* when Watson came home.

"How is she?" I asked. I wasn't sure what to call Watson's ex-wife. I didn't even know her name.

"At home and on her feet," he replied. "Or at any rate, on her foot. She's okay. But you guys," he said to Karen, "are going to stay with me for the rest of the weekend so Mommy can rest, okay?"

"Goody!" said Karen.

"How did everybody get along?" asked Watson.

"Fine," I answered. Suddenly I felt shy.

"Daddy, I like Kristy," Karen announced. "I don't mind if she's going to be our step-sister."

Watson smiled, but I blushed. "Well, I'm glad everything went so well," he said.

"Does she have to go home now?" asked Karen.

"Well, she won't be able to if Andrew is asleep. Is he napping?"

"He went down about —" I checked my watch — "almost an hour ago."

"Hmm," said Watson. "I don't really want

to wake him up. Do you want to call your mom and have her pick you up?"

"I better not," I said. "She probably won't want to leave David Michael."

"Do you mind waiting? Andrew shouldn't sleep more than another half hour or so."

"I don't mind." And I didn't. I really didn't. While we waited for Andrew, Watson took turns playing checkers with Karen and me. He won every game. I was glad because if he'd *let* me win, it would have proved he was trying too hard to make us feel like one big happy family.

Later, as Watson was driving me home, Karen said, "Kristy, I wish you were our big stepsister, right now."

"Well," I said, "how about if I be your baby-sitter instead?"

"That's okay," said Karen.

"Yeah, that's okay," echoed Andrew.

I glanced at Watson. He was sneaking a look at me, too. We smiled at each other.

That night after Mom had gotten David Michael to sleep, she came into my room. I was writing up my experience at Watson's in the Baby-sitters Club Notebook.

"So," she said, "now that we have a moment to ourselves, tell me how everything went at

Watson's. I'm sorry that was thrown at you today, but maybe it worked out for the best."

I was glad Mom wasn't saying, I told you so.

"It went okay," I said. "Andrew and Karen are cute. Andrew hardly ever talks, though. Karen says the divorce upsets him."

"It does upset him," Mom said, "but he's also got a big talker for an older sister. He almost doesn't *need* to speak."

"Karen sure is a big talker," I agreed. "I think she's really smart."

"She is. She just started kindergarten, and her teacher is already thinking of putting her in first grade after Christmas."

"Wow," I said.

"Kristy, would you baby-sit for Watson's children again, if he needed you?"

"I already told Karen that since I couldn't be her stepsister yet, at least I'd be her baby-sitter."

My mother looked pleased.

"Mom?" I asked. "What will happen when you and Watson get married? I mean, *if* you get married. Would Andrew and Karen live with us? Would we all live in Watson's house? It's so big."

"Does it bother you that there are no arrangements yet?"

"Yes," I replied. "I like to know what's going to happen."

"I'm afraid I can't tell you anything definite, honey."

"Can you tell me something *un*definite?"

Mom smiled. "Well, first of all, Watson's custody arrangements probably won't change, so wherever we live, Andrew and Karen won't live with us. They'll only visit. And right now, it looks as though we might move to Watson's, simply because there's more space."

"But I don't want to move!"

"Kristy, I said 'might.' "

"Okay."

"Time to get ready for bed now. Good-night, sweetheart."

" 'Night, Mom."

CHAPTER 14

On Monday at our next meeting of the Baby-sitters Club, everyone seemed to be back to normal. And most of us had news.

"Guess what!" Mary Anne said, in between phone calls.

"What?" Claudia and Stacey and I said.

"Dad and I hardly talked to each other all day Saturday, but on Sunday, I decided to go ahead and try reasoning with him about the money I earn, since I figured I didn't have anything to lose. I told him I'd be earning a lot of money through the Baby-sitters Club, and I asked him if I could spend half of it any way I wanted — *if* I promised to put the other half in the bank. And he said yes! So if we have the party, I can go!"

"Great!" I cried. "Hey, that's wonderful! You really stood up to your dad."

"Yeah. . . ." Mary Anne looked embarrassed, but I knew she was pleased with herself.

"I have some good news, too," Claudia said. "I caught up on almost all of my homework, and I got a B-minus on those ten math problems. *And* last night *I* had a talk with *my* parents. I told them I wasn't Janine and they said they knew that. Then they said I had to start setting aside time for my homework every day. At first I thought Dad was going to say no more baby-sitting, but instead he said an hour or so after dinner would be all right, and he and Mom and Janine and Mimi would help me. That cuts into my TV time, but I'd rather give up TV than art or baby-sitting and the club." Claudia reached under her mattress and pulled out some licorice sticks, which of course she passed around and of course Stacey refused.

"Well, that's good," said Mary Anne. "I'm proud of us, aren't you, Claudia?"

"Yeah," said Claudia.

I wanted to tell my good news about sitting for Watson's kids, but I was more curious about Stacey and why she had done what she did.

"So, Stace," I said brightly. "How was your weekend? How was New York?"

"Oh, it was fine. I went shopping at Bloomingdale's and bought this." She indicated the plaid wool pants she was wearing, which were held up with bright red suspenders. "I got a matching hat, too."

"Nice," I said. "How were your friends?"

"Fine." Stacey was picking at a piece of fuzz on her pants, carefully not looking at the rest of us.

"It must have been fun to spend so much time with them."

"Yeah."

"You know, the strangest thing happened on Saturday morning," I said. As usual, I couldn't help it. I was dying to say what I knew. There would be no stopping me, despite the fact that Claudia was sending me an urgent telegram with her eyes. *Shut up*, they were saying. *Don't do this.* But it was too late, even though I knew it was going to cause problems. Even though I knew that Claudia still considered Mary Anne and me babies, and Stacey sophisticated, and therefore was going to protect Stacey and whatever she was up to.

"Mary Anne saw you come home with your parents on Saturday," I said. "How come you made your mom say you stayed in New York?"

Stacey's head jerked up, her eyes flashing. She looked like she wanted to kill Mary Anne or me or possibly both of us. "Are you accusing my mom of lying?" she cried.

I thought for a moment. "I guess so."

Stacey stood up, hands on her hips. "Kristy, you — you — "

See, the thing is, right then, if Stacey wanted an "out," she had one. She could have blamed the whole thing on her mother by saying her mother was punishing her that weekend or something, and boy, weren't parents awful. But she didn't do that. She just blew up. And she didn't give any reason for why she and her mom were lying, which, Mary Anne said later to me in private, only proved that Stacey (and her mother) were covering something up.

Anyway, Stacey stood in Claudia's room, glowering at me. "I can't believe you just said that, Kristy. You're such a baby."

"You don't have any tact at all," added Claudia, immediately jumping to Stacey's defense, as I had known she would.

Mary Anne remained silent. She hates arguments.

"Well, how do you think I feel, being lied to?" I shouted. "Talk about tact. It made me feel like a little kid."

"You *are* a little kid," said Claudia. "Look at how you're dressed."

I looked. "What's wrong with the way I'm dressed?"

"Really, Kristy, a sweater with snowflakes and snowmen on it? You look like a four-year-old."

"Well, *you've* got sheep barrettes in your hair," I yelled. "You think they're adult?"

"Sheep," Claudia informed me witheringly, "are *in*."

"Who cares? Everything's in *some*time. First it was frogs, then pigs, now it's sheep. Maybe next week it'll be snowmen. And how do you expect me to keep up with that stuff, anyway? I don't have time for it."

"That's because you and Mary Anne are too busy playing dolls."

"*Dolls!*" I yelled. (Mary Anne looked as if she'd been slapped in the face. I knew she was going to start crying soon, and it only made me angrier.) *"We do not play with dolls!"* The thing is, though, that we just gave them up over the summer.

At that moment, surprisingly, Mary Anne spoke up. "Claudia, Kristy didn't mean to upset Stacey." Mary Anne's chin was trembling. Her eyes were about to overflow.

"Didn't mean to upset her! She accused her mother of lying."

Mary Anne's eyes spilled over.

"Oh, what a crybaby," Claudia said, but I could see she felt bad.

Suddenly a knock came on the door.

"What!" yelled Claudia.

The door opened a crack. I was terrified that Janine was going to be on the other side of it with some stupid comment like there's no such word as *crybaby*.

But it was Mimi who poked her head in. "Excuse me, girls," said Claudia's grand-mother in her gentle, slightly accented voice, "but what is going on in here? Downstairs I can hear you. You are yelling. What is wrong, and may I help you in some way?"

We all grew quiet. I felt slightly ashamed. "I'm sorry, Mimi," said Claudia. We'd all been standing up about ready to kill each other, and now we found places to sit down again.

"Are you girls all right? May I help?" Mimi asked again.

"No, thank you," said Claudia, sounding subdued. "We didn't mean to be so loud."

"All right. If you need me, I will be in the kitchen. Claudia, your friends must leave in fifteen minutes."

"Okay."

Mimi tiptoed out and closed the door softly behind her. I looked at the four of us and saw

136

that we were sitting as if we were at war: Mary Anne next to me on the floor, Claudia and Stacey together on the bed. We were facing off.

The phone rang.

"I'll get it," we all said, and leaped for the phone, each of us determined to answer it. Stacey and I got to it first and both grabbed it off the hook. We had a real tug-of-war, yanking it back and forth, before I jerked it out of Stacey's grip.

"Baby-sitters Club," I said gruffly. "Yes? . . . Yes?" It was a new client. He needed a sitter for Thursday after school for his seven-year-old daughter. I took down all the information, and said that I'd get back to him in five minutes.

"Well?" said Claudia after I'd hung up the phone.

Stacey was so mad she had turned red. No kidding. She couldn't even speak.

"Who's free Thursday afternoon?" I asked. "It's a seven-year-old kid, Charlotte Johanssen, on Kimball Street."

"I'm free," said Claudia.

"So'm I," Stacey managed to say through clenched teeth.

"Me, too," said Mary Anne timidly.

"Me, too," I added.

We glared at one another.

"Well, now what?" said Stacey.

"Yeah." Claudia narrowed her eyes. "Whose dumb idea was this club, anyway? Four people all wanting the same job. That's stupid."

"Since the club was *my* dumb idea," I snapped, "*I'll* take the stupid job." And I did. After I'd hung up the phone for the second time I said to Mary Anne, "Come on, let's go. I can see we're not wanted *here*."

Claudia looked a bit sheepish. "Kristy . . ." she said hesitantly.

"Save it. I'm not speaking to you at the moment."

Mary Anne and I left the house without bothering to say good-bye to Mimi. Mary Anne was crying again. I almost said something nasty to her, but realized that if I did, the four of us might become three against one, which was definitely worse than two against two.

"Don't cry," I said at last.

"I'm sorry. I just hate fighting, that's all."

"Me, too. But we'll all be friends again soon."

"I guess so."

"I know so. We've got the club to hold us together, right?"

"Right," agreed Mary Anne.

But she didn't sound very sure, and I didn't feel very sure.

* * *

So even though I was worried about the fight and sorry we'd had it, I believed that it would all blow over soon enough. And by later that evening, I heard such astonishing news that I forgot all about the fight anyway.

Mom and Watson had gone out to dinner, and my brothers and I had finished our homework and were sitting around the kitchen table playing Monopoly. Well, Charlie and Sam and I were playing Monopoly. David Michael, who had fully recovered from his virus, was busy making G.I. Joe attack a ferocious enemy Kleenex box. Sam had just bought all four railroads and was cleaning Charlie and me out, when the back door opened and in walked Mom and Watson. We hadn't expected them home so early.

"Surprise!" cried Mom, coming into the kitchen. Watson threw a handful of confetti on her.

My brothers and I smiled. "What's going on?" asked Charlie.

Mom and Watson looked at each other, eyes sparkling.

I got a funny feeling in the pit of my stomach.

"You tell them," said Watson.

Mom turned to us. She looked radiant. "I agreed to become engaged," she said.

Already?

Mom held up her left hand. There was a ring on her fourth finger with a diamond on it about the size of a boulder.

"Wow," I couldn't help saying.

We all crowded around to look at the ring. "It's pretty," said David Michael.

"It means Watson is going to be your step-daddy," Mom told him.

"Really-really-really?" David Michael jumped up and down. Sam hugged Mom, and Charlie shook Watson's hand. But I just stood there. I wasn't upset, but I wasn't happy either. I could only think of questions. Finally, I asked just one. "When will the wedding be?"

"Oh, not for months," replied Mom.

I let out a sigh. That was definitely a relief.

CHAPTER 15

On Tuesday, Mary Anne and I avoided Claudia and Stacey in school until the very end of the day. Then I screwed up the nerve to ask Claudia if she wanted to hold a Baby-sitters Club meeting the next day as usual. She said it was all right with her.

That night, for a change, Mom and my brothers and I went over to Watson's for dinner. Andrew and Karen were there. Watson was taking care of them more often than usual since their mother had broken her ankle.

Karen was in rare form. She loved having company and spent a long time trying to straighten out all the relationships. "If my daddy and your mommy get married — " she started to say to me, hopping from one foot to the other while Watson passed a plate of potato chips and onion dip around the living room.

"*When* we get married," Watson interrupted her.

"Okay, *when* you get married, Kristy, you'll be my stepsister, and Charlie, you'll be my biggest stepbrother. . . . How old are you, anyway?"

"Guess," said Charlie.

"Thirty-five?"

That broke Charlie up. "Thirty-*five!* That's practically over the — "

"Watch what you say, young man," said Mom. "If thirty-five is over the hill, then I better start shopping for Geritol and Dentu-Grip."

Everyone laughed.

"Twenty-nine?" Karen guessed.

"No!" said Charlie. "I'm sixteen."

Karen stared at him. "Okay," she said at last. She turned to Sam. "You'll be my next biggest stepbrother."

"Yeah, and you know how old I am? A hundred and twelve."

I giggled. So did Karen.

"And you'll be my last stepbrother," she said to David Michael. (It was a good thing she hadn't said "my littlest stepbrother.")

"Do you know how old I am?" he asked.

I hoped Karen was more accurate with little

people than big ones, because David Michael is very touchy about his age. He hates for people to think he's younger than six.

"Eight?"

I breathed a sigh of relief. David Michael beamed.

"Want to see my room?" Karen asked him.

"Sure!"

David Michael and Karen ran up the stairs, with Andrew at their heels.

I sat back in my chair and looked around the living room. There was no carpet, just little throw rugs with the wooden floor, all polished, in between. In one corner of the room was a small tree in a brass tub. At one end was a huge fireplace. Near the other end was a gleaming grand piano. I decided I liked the room. I decided I could get used to it if I had to.

Dinner was fun. Watson made fondue. He set a big pot full of hot, melty cheese in the middle of the table. Then he gave everyone a long fork and a plate of pieces of French bread. You were supposed to spear a piece of bread with your fork, dip it in the cheese, and eat it. Watson made this rule that if your bread fell off your fork and landed in the cheese, you had to kiss the person sitting on your right.

"Ew! Yuck!" said David Michael.

Then everyone began making rules. "If you drip cheese on the tablecloth," said Charlie, "you can't eat for two minutes."

"If you knock someone's bread off his fork, you become his slave for the evening," I said.

Everyone was really careful after that.

And then it happened. I was just sticking my fork into the pot when my bread fell off and landed in the cheese. Guess who was on my right. Watson.

I couldn't even look up. Maybe no one had noticed what I'd done.

But *every*one had.

"Oo-ooh, Kris-*teee*," teased Sam.

"Kiss Daddy, kiss Daddy!" cried Karen.

I glanced across the table and saw Mom watching me. I bet she thought I wouldn't do it, that I'd make a scene. Well, I'd show her.

I leaned over, gave Watson a peck on the cheek that was so fast you probably couldn't even have timed it, and went back to my dinner.

Later, when we were cleaning up the kitchen, I began to feel a little guilty. I mean, I could have been nicer about the kiss. So I sneaked into the den, found a piece of paper, and wrote Watson this note:

Dear Watson,

The next time you need a baby-sitter for Andrew and Karen, please call me first. I would be happy to do the job.

Yours truly,
Kristy

P.S. The fondue was fun.
P.P.S. I like your house.
P.P.P.S. If you and Mom want to get married, it's okay with me.

I almost wrote "Love, Kristy" then, but I didn't want to get mushy, so I didn't say anything else. I taped the note to Watson's bathroom mirror.

The next day, Mary Anne and I walked to Claudia's house for the club meeting. We went together, sort of as protection. When we reached Claudia's room, we found her talking to Stacey. When we entered, the talking stopped. Silence.

Mary Anne and I sat down. I was determined not to be the first one to speak, since I felt I had already made an effort by asking whether we were going to hold a meeting that day.

At long last, Claudia said, "I'm sorry I was so mean yesterday. I'm sorry I yelled." She was looking at Mary Anne, but not at me.

"That's okay," said Mary Anne.

"And I'm sorry I lied," said Stacey.

"Claudia, are you only sorry about making Mary Anne cry, or are you also sorry you yelled at *me*?" I asked.

Claudia sighed. "Kristy," she said, "I'm sorry I lost my temper. I really am. I had no reason to yell at Mary Anne, but *you* made me angry."

"How?" I demanded.

"You know how."

I looked at the floor. "By butting into someone else's business. By opening my mouth."

"Yeah."

"Well, I *did* tell a lie," said Stacey.

"But your lie didn't hurt anybody," said Claudia. "At least, as far as I know. And you must have had a good reason for lying, especially since your mom went along with you. Whatever it was, Kristy shouldn't have accused you like she did. It was just plain rude. You're my friend, and I don't want anyone to hurt you."

"But I'm your friend, too," I said.

"Right," agreed Claudia. "And I don't like my friends to be rude. If you weren't my friend, I wouldn't bother to tell you this. If you weren't my friend, you wouldn't be worth getting mad at."

I thought that over. "I have one thing to say about being lied to. I don't like it. And I have a right to say so." I had a feeling we weren't going to clear up the business of Stacey's lie, and that bothered me. But it was time to smooth things over. "I have something else to say, too. I'm really going to try to watch my mouth from now on. I mean it. My mouth gets me in trouble all the time. Just ask my mother."

"Just ask anybody," said Claudia.

We all giggled.

"Once, right after my grandmother came back from the beauty shop, I asked her why she had had her hair dyed purple," I said. "I was really in trouble then."

"Once I cried in front of my whole class," Mary Anne admitted.

"Oh, that's so embarrassing for a little kid," said Stacey knowingly.

"Little kid! It was last week!"

More giggling.

Then the phone rang and we got down to business.

At six o'clock I said, "I've got a great idea! Now that we've all straightened out our problems, I think we should try to have the pizza party again. Stace, you *really* don't have to worry about your diet. We can get you a salad at the pizza place, if you don't want pizza. They make really good salads."

"All right," she said slowly.

"And," I added, thinking of Stacey and Sam, "we can have the party at my house."

Stacey's eyes lit up. "O-*kay!* I'll be there."

"Is Saturday all right with everyone?" I asked.

We settled on Saturday at five o'clock. In the back of my mind, I was thinking that maybe I could talk Mom into a slumber party, and five seemed like a good hour for a sleep-over to begin.

Mom was easily talked into a slumber party. She liked the Baby-sitters Club. "After all," she told me, "it brought you and Watson closer together."

I nodded. "The club has helped all of us. It helped Stacey make some friends. I think it helped give Mary Anne the courage to stand up to her father. And it showed Claudia that she can be good at something besides art, even if it's not a genius kind of thing like Janine's good at." I was pretty pleased with our club, and I was glad Mom was pleased, too.

On Saturday at five o'clock, Mary Anne,

Claudia, and Stacey came over to my house, and our fabulous pizza-slumber party began. We ate and ate and ate. Well, Claudia and Mary Anne and I ate. Stacey had a helping of salad and an apple, and later in the evening she drank a diet soda and even joined the rest of us in some popcorn.

At eleven we put on our nightgowns and spread our sleeping bags out on the floor of the bedroom. Stacey had a really spectacular nightshirt with gold glitter and the skyline of New York City across the front.

"Gosh," said Mary Anne, "you are so lucky to have lived in New York, and to get to take trips there all the time. I've only been twice."

Stacey pressed her fingers together. She closed her eyes for a moment, then opened them and said, "You guys, I have something to tell you."

"What," I said eagerly. It sounded like a big confession was coming up.

Claudia gave me a look that said, Watch what you say.

I closed my mouth.

"I have a secret," Stacey began.

It was all I could do not to cry out, "I knew it! I knew you were hiding something."

"You know the diet I'm on? Well, it's not just any old diet. And the trips to New York?

They're not just to visit friends. I have to go to a doctor there. Sometimes I have to stay in the hospital overnight."

Claudia and Mary Anne looked stricken. "Oh, Stace," I said softly. "I knew it. You have anorexia, right? That's what the crazy diet is all about."

"Anorexia?" repeated Stacey. "No."

No?

"I have — I have diabetes," she managed to say. "I just got it last year."

Mary Anne opened her eyes wide.

"Oh, poor Stacey," said Claudia, giving her an awkward hug.

But I said, "Diabetes? Is *that* all?"

"Is that *all*?" exclaimed Stacey. "What do you mean?"

"Well, I mean . . . why didn't you just tell us? My cousin Robin has diabetes. It means you have a problem with sugar. Your body doesn't process it the way most people's bodies do. Too much or too little sugar can be dangerous, right? And you probably have to give yourself insulin shots every day. It's rotten, but I mean, you're not a freak or something. We'll quit offering you candy, okay?"

Claudia gave me another look. This one meant, sincerely, Good going, Kristy.

"But don't you guys care?" asked Stacey.

"Of course we care," I replied.

"I mean, doesn't it bother you?"

"No. Why should it?" said Claudia, frowning.

"Yeah," said Mary Anne and I.

"I don't know. My mother acts like it's some kind of curse. The kids at my old school started teasing me about my diet, and because I fainted a couple of times, so Mom decided we should come to a 'peaceful little town.' You know, get me to some place 'civilized and quiet.' "

"That's why you moved here?" said Mary Anne incredulously.

Stacey nodded. "Well, partly."

"Wow," I said.

"So I thought maybe I should cover up what was wrong with me. Moving here seemed like a chance to start over. But *not* telling you guys was worse than *tell*ing my old friends. It got so complicated with the lies and everything."

"Well," said Mary Anne in her quiet way, "maybe you don't have to tell *all* the kids. We know, and that's important because we see you most often. Maybe you could sort of keep quiet about it at school — but not lie about it."

"That's true," agreed Stacey. Her face softened. "You guys are great."

We smiled.

"I think we should have a slumber party

once a month," she exclaimed.

"Yeah," I said. "When Mom and Watson get married, we'll have them at Watson's house, if we move there. The third floor would be perfect. We could have it all to ourselves."

"When your mother and Watson get *married!*" cried Claudia.

I nodded. Then I told my friends everything.

Just as I was finishing, a knock came on the door. "Hey, all you girls!" called Sam's voice. "Mom said to bring this to you. Don't worry, I'm not coming in. I'm leaving it outside the door. Now I'm walking down the hall. Now I'm going down the stairs. . . ." His footsteps faded away.

I opened the door and found a tray with four glasses, a bottle of diet soda, an apple, a package of cookies, and a note from Mom that said she left lots of food so we wouldn't have to raid the refrigerator.

I brought the tray inside.

"Your brother's so cute, Kristy," said Stacey.

"I guess. For a boy."

"No, really. . . . Do you like any boys, Kristy?"

I made a face.

"What do — " Stacey started to say, but I held my finger to my lips.

"Shh!" I hissed. "Do you hear that?"

"What?"

"Something at the window."

We made ourselves quiet. We couldn't hear a sound.

"I guess it's nothing," I said. But while we were all in the mood, I turned out the lights and whispered to the others, "What's the scariest thing that ever happened while you were baby-sitting?"

In hushed voices we began telling about creepy nights sitting up in silent houses, waiting for parents to come home. Then we started telling ghost stories.

I felt deliciously scared — and happy. We were friends again. Things were okay with Watson. The Baby-sitters Club was a success. I, Kristin Amanda Thomas, had made it work, or helped to make it work. I hoped that Mary Anne, Claudia, Stacey, and I — the Baby-sitters Club — would stay together for a long time.

Dear Reader,

Now that you've read *Kristy's Great Idea*, I thought you might like to know a little bit about how this story and the Baby-sitters Club came to be.

In 1985 I had just left my job and started to write books for kids full-time. That was when my editor suggested that I write a four-book mini-series entitled "The Baby-sitters Club." I had to figure out what a baby-sitters club might be, and decided on a business run by a group of friends. Then I created Kristy, Claudia, Stacey, and Mary Anne. I wanted to create a group of kids who are very different from each other but work well together. I based Kristy on my best friend from when I was growing up, and Mary Anne on me. Kristy was the outgoing one with all the big ideas, and Mary Anne was the quiet one. She and Kristy were best friends even though they were opposites. Eventually Claudia and Stacey would become best friends, too.

Baby-sitting was easy for me to write about because I did so much of it when I was growing up. (In fact, right through college.) So I thought I would enjoy writing about it, too. And I do!

Happy reading,

Ann M. Martin

L. GODWIN

Ann M. Martin

About the Author

ANN MATTHEWS MARTIN was born on August 12, 1955. She grew up in Princeton, NJ, with her parents and her younger sister, Jane.

Although Ann used to be a teacher and then an editor of children's books, she's now a full-time writer. She gets ideas for her books from many different places. Some are based on personal experiences. Others are based on childhood memories and feelings. Many are written about contemporary problems or events.

All of Ann's characters, even the members of the Baby-sitters Club, are made up. (So is Stoneybrook.) But many of her characters are based on real people. Sometimes Ann names her characters after people she knows; other times she chooses names she likes.

In addition to the Baby-sitters Club books, Ann Martin has written many other books for children. Her favorite is *Ten Kids, No Pets* because she loves big families and she loves animals. Her favorite BSC book is *Kristy's Big Day.* (Kristy is her favorite baby-sitter.)

Ann M. Martin now lives in New York with her cats, Gussie, Woody, and Willy, and her dog, Sadie. Her hobbies are reading, sewing, and needlework — especially making clothes for children.

Notebook Pages

This Baby-sitters Club book belongs to _____ .

I am _____ years old and in the _____ grade.

The name of my school is _____ .

I got this BSC book from _____ .

I started reading it on _____ and

finished reading it on _____ .

The place where I read most of this book is _____ .

My favorite part was when _____ .

If I could change anything in the story, it might be the part when

_____ .

My favorite character in the Baby-sitters Club is _____ .

The BSC member I am most like is _____

because _____ .

If I could write a Baby-sitters Club book it would be about ____

_____

_____ .

#1 Kristy's Great Idea

Kristy had a great idea to start the Baby-sitters Club. If I were going to start a club it would be called _____ .

The purpose of my club would be to _____

_____ .

My club would do things like _____

_____ .

These are the people I would invite to be in my club:

_____ , President _____ , Secretary

_____ , Vice-President _____ , Treasurer

Other club members: _____ .

My club logo might look like this:

The Baby-sitters Club holds its meetings in Claudia's bedroom.

My club would meet _____ .

KRISTY'S

Playing softball with some of my favorite sitting charges.

A gab-fest

Me, age 3. Already on the go.

SCRAPBOOK

...with Mary Anne!

My family keeps growing!

David Michael, me, and Louie — the best dog ever.

Illustrations by Angelo Tillery

Read all the books about Kristy
in the Baby-sitters Club series
by Ann M. Martin

Mysteries:

4   *Kristy and the Missing Child*
           Kristy organizes a search party to help the police
           find a missing child.

9   *Kristy and the Haunted Mansion*
           Kristy and the Krashers are spending the night
           in a spooky old house!

15   *Kristy and the Vampires*
           A vampire movie is being shot in Stoneybrook.
           Can Kristy and the BSC find out who's out
           to get the star?

19   *Kristy and the Missing Fortune*
           It could all be Kristy's — if she and the BSC
           crack the case.

25   *Kristy and the Middle School Vandal*
           Cary Retlin is up to his old tricks — and Kristy
           has to stop him!

30   *Kristy and the Mystery Train*
           Kristy is in for the scariest ride of her life!

36   *Kristy and the Cat Burglar*
           Kristy is in the center of a mysterious theft.

Portrait Collection:

Kristy's Book
           The official autobiography of Kristin Amanda Thomas.

Collect them all!

❑ MG43388-1	#1	Kristy's Great Idea	$3.50
❑ MG43387-3	#10	Logan Likes Mary Anne!	$3.99
❑ MG43717-8	#15	Little Miss Stoneybrook...and Dawn	$3.50
❑ MG43722-4	#20	Kristy and the Walking Disaster	$3.50
❑ MG43347-4	#25	Mary Anne and the Search for Tigger	$3.50
❑ MG42498-X	#30	Mary Anne and the Great Romance	$3.50
❑ MG42508-0	#35	Stacey and the Mystery of Stoneybrook	$3.50
❑ MG44082-9	#40	Claudia and the Middle School Mystery	$3.25
❑ MG43574-4	#45	Kristy and the Baby Parade	$3.50
❑ MG44969-9	#50	Dawn's Big Date	$3.50
❑ MG44968-0	#51	Stacey's Ex-Best Friend	$3.50
❑ MG44966-4	#52	Mary Anne + 2 Many Babies	$3.50
❑ MG44967-2	#53	Kristy for President	$3.25
❑ MG44965-6	#54	Mallory and the Dream Horse	$3.25
❑ MG44964-8	#55	Jessi's Gold Medal	$3.25
❑ MG45657-1	#56	Keep Out, Claudia!	$3.50
❑ MG45658-X	#57	Dawn Saves the Planet	$3.50
❑ MG45659-8	#58	Stacey's Choice	$3.50
❑ MG45660-1	#59	Mallory Hates Boys (and Gym)	$3.50
❑ MG45662-8	#60	Mary Anne's Makeover	$3.50
❑ MG45663-6	#61	Jessi and the Awful Secret	$3.50
❑ MG45664-4	#62	Kristy and the Worst Kid Ever	$3.50
❑ MG45665-2	#63	Claudia's ~~Freind~~ Friend	$3.50
❑ MG45666-0	#64	Dawn's Family Feud	$3.50
❑ MG45667-9	#65	Stacey's Big Crush	$3.50
❑ MG47004-3	#66	Maid Mary Anne	$3.50
❑ MG47005-1	#67	Dawn's Big Move	$3.50
❑ MG47006-X	#68	Jessi and the Bad Baby-sitter	$3.50
❑ MG47007-8	#69	Get Well Soon, Mallory!	$3.50
❑ MG47008-6	#70	Stacey and the Cheerleaders	$3.50
❑ MG47009-4	#71	Claudia and the Perfect Boy	$3.99
❑ MG47010-8	#72	Dawn and the We ❤ Kids Club	$3.99
❑ MG47011-6	#73	Mary Anne and Miss Priss	$3.99
❑ MG47012-4	#74	Kristy and the Copycat	$3.99
❑ MG47013-2	#75	Jessi's Horrible Prank	$3.50
❑ MG47014-0	#76	Stacey's Lie	$3.50
❑ MG48221-1	#77	Dawn and Whitney, Friends Forever	$3.99
❑ MG48222-X	#78	Claudia and Crazy Peaches	$3.50
❑ MG48223-8	#79	Mary Anne Breaks the Rules	$3.50
❑ MG48224-6	#80	Mallory Pike, #1 Fan	$3.99
❑ MG48225-4	#81	Kristy and Mr. Mom	$3.50
❑ MG48226-2	#82	Jessi and the Troublemaker	$3.99
❑ MG48235-1	#83	Stacey vs. the BSC	$3.50
❑ MG48228-9	#84	Dawn and the School Spirit War	$3.50
❑ MG48236-X	#85	Claudi Kishi, Live from WSTO	$3.50
❑ MG48227-0	#86	Mary Anne and Camp BSC	$3.50
❑ MG48237-8	#87	Stacey and the Bad Girls	$3.50
❑ MG22872-2	#88	Farewell, Dawn	$3.50

More titles... ▶

❑ MG22873-0	#89	**Kristy and the Dirty Diapers**	$3.50
❑ MG22874-9	#90	**Welcome to the BSC, Abby**	$3.99
❑ MG22875-1	#91	**Claudia and the First Thanksgiving**	$3.50
❑ MG22876-5	#92	**Mallory's Christmas Wish**	$3.50
❑ MG22877-3	#93	**Mary Anne and the Memory Garden**	$3.99
❑ MG22878-1	#94	**Stacey McGill, Super Sitter**	$3.99
❑ MG22879-X	#95	**Kristy + Bart = ?**	$3.99
❑ MG22880-3	#96	**Abby's Lucky Thirteen**	$3.99
❑ MG22881-1	#97	**Claudia and the World's Cutest Baby**	$3.99
❑ MG22882-X	#98	**Dawn and Too Many Sitters**	$3.99
❑ MG69205-4	#99	**Stacey's Broken Heart**	$3.99
❑ MG69206-2	#100	**Kristy's Worst Idea**	$3.99
❑ MG69207-0	#101	**Claudia Kishi, Middle School Dropout**	$3.99
❑ MG69208-9	#102	**Mary Anne and the Little Princess**	$3.99
❑ MG69209-7	#103	**Happy Holidays, Jessi**	$3.99
❑ MG69210-0	#104	**Abby's Twin**	$3.99
❑ MG69211-9	#105	**Stacey the Math Whiz**	$3.99
❑ MG69212-7	#106	**Claudia, Queen of the Seventh Grade**	$3.99
❑ MG69213-5	#107	**Mind Your Own Business, Kristy!**	$3.99
❑ MG69214-3	#108	**Don't Give Up, Mallory**	$3.99
❑ MG69215-1	#109	**Mary Anne to the Rescue**	$3.99
❑ MG05988-2	#110	**Abby the Bad Sport**	$3.99
❑ MG05989-0	#111	**Stacey's Secret Friend**	$3.99
❑ MG05990-4	#112	**Kristy and the Sister War**	$3.99
❑ MG45575-3		**Logan's Story Special Edition Readers' Request**	$3.25
❑ MG47118-X		**Logan Bruno, Boy Baby-sitter**	
		Special Edition Readers' Request	$3.50
❑ MG47756-0		**Shannon's Story Special Edition**	$3.50
❑ MG47686-6		**The Baby-sitters Club Guide to Baby-sitting**	$3.25
❑ MG47314-X		**The Baby-sitters Club Trivia and Puzzle Fun Book**	$2.50
❑ MG48400-1		**BSC Portrait Collection: Claudia's Book**	$3.50
❑ MG22864-1		**BSC Portrait Collection: Dawn's Book**	$3.50
❑ MG69181-3		**BSC Portrait Collection: Kristy's Book**	$3.99
❑ MG22865-X		**BSC Portrait Collection: Mary Anne's Book**	$3.99
❑ MG48399-4		**BSC Portrait Collection: Stacey's Book**	$3.50
❑ MG69182-1		**BSC Portrait Collection: Abby's Book**	$3.99
❑ MG92713-2		**The Complete Guide to The Baby-sitters Club**	$4.95
❑ MG47151-1		**The Baby-sitters Club Chain Letter**	$14.95
❑ MG48295-5		**The Baby-sitters Club Secret Santa**	$14.95
❑ MG45074-3		**The Baby-sitters Club Notebook**	$2.50
❑ MG44783-1		**The Baby-sitters Club Postcard Book**	$4.95

Available wherever you buy books...or use this order form.
Scholastic Inc., P.O. Box 7502, Jefferson City, MO 65102

Please send me the books I have checked above. I am enclosing $_____
(please add $2.00 to cover shipping and handling). Send check or money order—
no cash or C.O.D.s please.

Name_____Birthdate_____

Address_____

City_____State/Zip_____

BSC5962